The
SOUND
of
SLEIGH
BELLS

Other Books by Cindy Woodsmall

The Hope of Refuge

When the Heart Cries

When the Morning Comes

When the Soul Mends

The
SOUND
of
SLEIGH
BELLS

CINDY
WOODSMALL

WATERBROOK
PRESS

THE SOUND OF SLEIGH BELLS
PUBLISHED BY WATERBROOK PRESS
12265 Oracle Boulevard, Suite 200
Colorado Springs, Colorado 80921

The scripture quoted on page 83 is taken from the Holy Bible, New International Version®. NIV®. Copyright © 1973, 1978, 1984 by International Bible Society. Used by permission of Zondervan Publishing House. All rights reserved. The scripture quoted on page 38 is taken from the King James Version.

The characters and events in this book are fictional, and any resemblance to actual persons or events is coincidental.

ISBN 978-0-307-44653-4
ISBN 978-0-307-45835-3 (electronic)

Published in the United States by WaterBrook Multnomah, an imprint of the Crown Publishing Group, a division of Random House Inc., New York.

WATERBROOK and its deer colophon are registered trademarks of Random House Inc.

Library of Congress Cataloging-in-Publication Data
Woodsmall, Cindy.
    The sound of sleigh bells / Cindy Woodsmall. — 1st ed.
        p. cm.
    ISBN 978-0-307-44653-4 — ISBN 978-0-307-45835-3 (electronic)
    1. Amish women—Fiction. I. Title.
    PS3623.O678S68 2009
    813'.6—dc22

                                        2009018239

Printed in the United States of America
2010

10 9 8 7 6 5

To one of the most splendid blessings in my life,
Miriam Flaud

One

The aroma of fresh-baked bread, shepherd's pie, and steamed vegetables filled Lizzy's house, mingling with the sweet smell of baked desserts. In the hearth a bank of embers kept a small fire burning, removing the nip that clung to the early-April air.

The noise of conversations rose and fell around Lizzy's kitchen table as her brother and his large family talked easily throughout the meal. His grown and almost-grown children filled the sides of her fourteen-foot table, and his grandchildren either sat in their mothers' laps or in highchairs.

Nearly four decades ago her oldest brother had put effort into finding an Amish bride. When Stephen found the right girl, he married her. He'd handled life well, and the fruit of it fed her soul. Lizzy had focused on her business and never married. She didn't regret her choices, not for herself, but she'd crawl on her hands and knees the rest of her days to keep her niece from the same fate.

Beth was like a daughter to Lizzy. Not long after the family's dry goods store passed to Lizzy, Beth graduated from the eighth grade and started working beside her. Soon she moved in with Lizzy, and they shared the one-bedroom apartment above the shop. When Lizzy had this house built a few years ago, her niece had stayed above Hertzlers' Dry Goods.

Lizzy studied the young beauty as she answered her family's endless questions about her decisions in the middleman role between the Amish who made goods and the various Englischer stores who wanted those goods.

That was her Beth. Answer what was asked. Do what was right. Always be polite. Offer to help before it was needed. And never let anyone see the grief that hadn't yet let go of her. Beth had banned even Lizzy from looking into the heartache that held her hostage.

The one-year anniversary of Henry's death had come and gone without any sign from Beth that she might lay aside her mourning, so Lizzy had taken action. She'd prepared this huge meal and planned a social for the afternoon. Maybe all Beth needed was a loving, gentle nudge. If not, Lizzy had a backup plan—one Beth would not appreciate.

Over the din of conversations, the sounds of horses and buggies arriving and the voices of young people drifted through the kitchen window, causing Beth to look at her.

Lizzy placed her forearms on the table. "I've invited the young singles of the community for an evening of outdoor games, desserts, and a bonfire when the sun goes down."

Two of Beth's single younger sisters, Fannie and Susie, glowed at the idea. With grace and gentleness, Beth turned to her *Mamm* and asked if she would need help planting this year's garden.

It didn't seem to bother Beth that five of her sisters had married before her, and three of them were younger than she was. All but the most recently wed had children. Lizzy knew what awaited Beth if she didn't find someone—awkward and never-ending loneliness. Maybe she didn't recognize that. It wasn't until Henry came into Beth's life that she even seemed to notice that single men existed. Within a year of meeting, they were making plans to marry.

Now, in an Amish community of dresses in rich, solid hues, Beth wore black.

Through a window Lizzy saw the young men bring their rigs to a halt. The drivers as well as the passengers got out of the carriages. The girls soon huddled in groups, talking feverishly, while the guys went into the barn, pulled two wagons with plenty of hay into the field, and tied their horses to them. It was far easier to leave the animals harnessed and grazing on hay than to have to hitch a horse to its buggy in the dark. The young people knew the routine. They would remain outside playing volleyball, horseshoes, or whatever else suited them until after the sun went down. Then they'd come inside for desserts and hot chocolate or coffee before riding in wagons to the field where they'd start a bonfire.

Fannie and Susie rose and began clearing the table. Beth went to the dessert counter and picked out a pie. She set it on the table beside her *Daed,* cut a slice, and placed it on his plate. Then she slid a piece onto her Mamm's plate before passing the pie to her brother Emmanuel. She took her seat next to her mother, still chatting about the upcoming spring planting. Lizzy hoped her brother saw what she did—a daughter who continued to shun all possibility of finding new love. Beth clung to the past as if she might wake one day to find her burning desires had changed it.

Fannie began gathering glasses that still held trace amounts of lemonade. "You've got to join us this time, Bethie. It's been too long."

Flatware stopped clinking against the plates as all eyes turned to Beth.

Susie tugged on her sleeve. "Please. Everyone misses you."

Beth poked at the meal she'd barely touched as if she might scoop a forkful of the cold food and eat it. "Not this time. *Denki.*"

"See, Beth," Lizzy said. "Every person here knows you should be out socializing again. Everyone except you."

Beth's face grew taut, and she stood and removed the small stack of plates from Fannie's hands. "Go on. I'll do these."

Fannie glanced to her Daed.

He nodded. "Why don't you all finish up and go on out? Emmanuel and Ira, do you mind helping set up the volleyball nets?"

Emmanuel wiped his mouth on a cloth napkin. "We can do that."

Chairs screeched against the wood floor as most of the brood stood. Fannie and Susie bolted for the door. Two more of Beth's sisters and two sisters-in-law went to the sink, taking turns rinsing the hands and faces of their little ones before they all went outside.

Lizzy longed to see Beth in colored dresses, wearing a smile that radiated from her soul. Instead Beth pasted on smiles, fooling most of those around her into thinking her heart continued to mend. But her quieter, more stoic behavior said things no one else seemed to hear. Lizzy heard, and she'd shared her concerns with Beth's Daed, Stephen.

Beth took a stack of dishes to the sink and flicked on the water.

"You can leave that for now," Stephen said.

She turned off the water and remained with her back to them.

Beth's Mamm glanced at Lizzy as she ran her finger down a tall glass of lemonade. "Beth, honey—"

Beth turned. "I'm fine, Mamm."

Stephen got up and piled more plates together. "Of course you are. And I'll throw my favorite pie at anyone who says otherwise." He stuck his finger into his half-eaten piece of chocolate pie, placed it in his mouth, and winked at Beth.

She smiled, an expression that probably looked real to her Daed but reminded Lizzy of fine silk flowers—only beautiful to those who aren't gardeners.

"Beth, sweetheart," Stephen said, "you know how me and your Mamm feel. We love you. It's no secret that you're different from our other girls. You've always had more of a head for business than a heart to find a beau, but now…well, we just want to make sure you're doing okay. Since you don't live with us, that's a bit hard to know sometimes." He set the dirty dishes beside the already full sink before he rinsed his hands and dried them. "Officially, your period of mourning was over nearly six months ago, but you haven't joined the young people for a single event. You've not left the store for your usual buying trips. You eat half of what you should. You continue to wear black. And those are things a stranger would notice."

"I…I could plan a buying-and-selling trip. It'll take me most of the summer to get completely organized for it, but I can be ready by August. I know I should have sooner, but…"

Lizzy hoped Stephen didn't fall for the diversion tactic Beth had just thrown his way, but since Beth was listening to him without getting defensive, Lizzy wouldn't interfere.

"Good. If that's where you feel like beginning, I'm glad to hear it. I know the community will be too, because without you they can't sell near as many of their goods." He walked to the table, took a seat, and motioned for Beth.

She moved to the chair beside him.

"But other people's financial needs are not what this is about. Tell me something good and hopeful about you—something I'll know in my gut is true—and I'll end this conversation right now."

The four of them remained silent as shouts and roars of laughter echoed from outside. If anyone could touch Beth's heart and cause her to change, her Daed could. But the silence continued, and Beth's inability to think of anything hopeful to say made Lizzy sick with worry.

The grandfather clock chimed the half hour, startling Lizzy, but no one spoke. Long shadows filled the room, and she lit a kerosene lamp and set it in the middle of the table.

Whatever happened the night Henry died consumed Beth. When Lizzy arrived on the scene, her niece didn't even acknowledge her. The only words Beth spoke were the ones she whispered for days—*God, forgive me.* Lizzy had tried to talk to her about it, but Beth never broke her polite silence on the topic.

Beth's Daed cleared his throat. "I'll wait all night for an answer if I need to, Beth."

Her eyes filled with tears, but it was another five minutes before she uttered a word. "I don't trust my feelings about…certain things anymore, Daed."

"Then can you trust mine?" her Daed asked.

"Always, but I don't want to be one of the single girls looking for a husband. Not ever again. Is that such a horrible thing?"

"It's not what we'd figured on, but we can adjust."

Lizzy repositioned her glass of lemonade. During church the singles sat separately from the married couples. Lizzy's memory of growing too old for the singles and removing herself from them still stung. From that day on she'd carried the title of *alt Maedel*—old maid. She'd been older than Beth's twenty-six years, and her prospects of finding someone had faded into nothingness. If Beth thought navigating life after Henry was difficult, Lizzy dreaded the pain that lay ahead for Beth when she openly admitted to the Amish world that she didn't fit—not with the single folk and not with the married ones.

Stephen had yet to mention anything about the color of mourning Beth still wore. If she would wear something besides black, young men would gravitate to her, and she stood a chance of finding someone.

He covered Beth's hand with his and bowed his head, silently praying for her. He lifted his head. "There's somewhere you'd like to be tonight other than washing dishes or working in that stuffy office in the store. Am I right?"

"*Ya.*"

"Then go."

Beth kissed her Daed's cheek, told her Mamm and Lizzy she'd see them later, and left.

Lizzy moved to the window and watched as her niece walked past small groups of young people. She overheard both women and men asking Beth to stay. Beth shook her head, smiled, and waved before making her way across the road and into the pasture near their store.

"You said nothing that will nudge her to change how she's handling life," Lizzy said.

Stephen placed his hands on her shoulders. "Henry's death is the hardest thing this family has faced. Pressuring Beth isn't the answer. Trusting God is."

Lizzy stood in silence as Beth harnessed her mare to a carriage. She knew where Beth was going.

The cemetery.

Again. And again. And again.

"Please, dear God, move a mountain for her."

Stephen squeezed her shoulders. "Amen."

Two

Sitting inside her small office, Beth could hear the bell above the door softly jingle each time a customer came in or went out of the store. But the stack of paperwork spread out in front of her was a clear reminder that helping to run Hertzlers' Dry Goods was only a small part of her work.

When dozens of wall clocks chimed the noon hour, Beth jolted. Her day was getting away from her. She grabbed a utility knife and opened the box beside her desk. It'd been delivered that morning and contained stacks of her catalogs from the printer. After pulling one out, she moved the kerosene lamp closer. The heat from the small flame added to late summer's soaring temperature, but she needed the extra light to view all the details of the ordering magazine. The photos were of almost every item she carried, and they looked fantastic.

Lizzy will love it.

Beth's practice in creating a periodical had paid off. A few years back she had gotten special permission from the church leaders to use a camera for the purpose of developing a sales publication. Her first few tries were very clumsy compared to this.

She organized the papers on her desk and shoved some into her satchel. With her itinerary, a catalog, and stacks of order forms in hand, she blew out the kerosene lamp and left her office. As she stepped into the dry goods store, she noticed customers in every aisle, Amish and Englischers. She'd been focused on her trip plans for months, and she finally took a moment to actually see the place. Lizzy ran the day-to-day operation of the store, and by the looks of it, she was having a particularly good season.

Beth went to the door that led to her living quarters. As she climbed the darkened stairwell, the well-worn steps moaned, and the aroma of old wood filled her senses. It made her wish for time to sit on the steps and just breathe it in. Even after she rounded the first landing of the stairway, she could hear the buzz of customers in the shop below. Some days she didn't feel Amish at all. She only felt busy and overwhelmed. It took a lot of Englischer-type work to provide middle-man services for a multitude of Amish districts, but she loved it.

"Beth?" one of the Petersheim girls called from the foot of the steps.

She stopped climbing and went back down the winding staircase. "Yes, Lillian?"

"Mr. Jenkins is here. He wants to place an order for his store."

"His appointment was last week, and he missed it. Does he think it's for today?"

Lillian moved to the first step and closed the door behind her. "No. He apologized for not being here when he should've. A family illness kept him away, but he's in the area today and hoping you'll let him place an order before you leave on your buying trip. I told him you're leaving in a couple of hours, but that only made him more determined."

"Okay, I'll take his order, but I need to finish packing first. Help him look through the catalog and the display room while he waits, and take really good notes. It'll speed things along. And please tell him I have to be gone by two o'clock."

Lillian nodded and left.

Beth turned and headed up the stairway. In spite of her best efforts, which began four months ago, she still had too much to do before leaving. Half a dozen calls had to be made, and she needed to sort through her mail before the driver arrived. Right now she intended to finish packing. It wouldn't do to leave without plenty of clean clothing. It was hard enough to earn respect among the Englischers as a businesswoman when wearing Amish clothing, let alone dirty Amish attire.

When she stepped into her attic bedroom, she expected a few minutes of solitude. Instead, she found her aunt going through her closet. Lizzy's youthful face and bustling energy kept her from looking twelve years older than Beth. Her aunt carried a couple more pounds of weight than she had a decade ago, and her dark hair had a few strands of gray, but Beth thought she looked much younger than her actual age of thirty-eight.

Lizzy motioned at the closet and then faced Beth. "Have you discarded every dress you own that isn't black?"

Beth lowered her eyes and studied the pages in her hand. Black hid things—much like ever-darkening shadows in a deep forest. And as odd as it seemed, black helped her carry things too.

Secret things.

She tapped the itinerary. "If I'm careful to stick to the schedule, before my three weeks are up, I'll be able to visit every Amish and Englischer store that we do business with—furniture, quilt, dolls, crafts—you name it. I have an appointment to see each owner, buyer, or manager we're connected to in Pennsylvania and Ohio." She held out the updated catalog.

"It arrived!" Lizzy stepped away from the closet and took the publication.

"I told you it was scheduled to get here this morning."

Her aunt's dark brown eyes reflected awe as she looked at each page. "Wow, Beth, this is the best one yet."

"The community has waited a long time for me to resume traveling, and I intend for this trip to be very successful." After setting the rest of the papers on her nightstand, Beth stepped around her aunt. She grabbed several dresses from her closet and tossed them onto the bed.

Lizzy removed the hangers and folded each dress. "Beth, honey..."

Beth swallowed, her mind racing with ideas of how to avoid the impending conversation—the one her aunt had started trying to have a few days ago. "Mr. Jenkins is waiting for me downstairs, and I have phone calls to make before Gloria arrives. Can you finish packing for me?"

Her aunt's frame slumped so slightly Beth doubted if Lizzy even knew it'd happened. After emptying a drawer of her dresser, Beth shoved the stockings and underwear into the traveling bag.

"Ya." Lizzy's brown eyes met Beth's, and her aunt smiled. "I know you wish you could change the past, but you have to let it go, Bethie."

Beth had no doubt her aunt thought she knew what dark cloud hung over her. But she was wrong.

Beth grabbed the papers from the nightstand and gave Lizzy a quick hug. "Don't start trying to mollycoddle me again. I think we can all agree that at twenty-six I'm a big girl now."

"And I'm thirty-eight, but that doesn't keep me from needing to hear what other people have to say."

"I've heard you, Lizzy. You're concerned, but you're not hearing me. I'm fine." She kissed her aunt. "Now help me with my list so I can get out the door on time."

Her aunt nodded. "I'll finish packing for you."

"Denki." Beth scurried downstairs.

Hoping to stay hidden so Lizzy couldn't start another difficult conversation, Beth gratefully donated the next hour of her life to helping Mr. Jenkins place an order, then made the necessary phone calls. After sorting her business mail, she was down to her last task—finding where she'd laid her personal mail. She'd seen it sometime last week, although she wasn't sure what day.

She stepped out of her office. "Hey, Lillian?"

Lillian looked up from the cash register, where she was checking out a customer.

"Have you seen a stack of six or seven letters with a rubber band around it?"

Lizzy came out of the storage room, reached under a nearby

counter, and smiled as she waved the envelopes in the air. "I wondered when you'd miss them."

Beth moved toward her aunt. "I realized they were missing this morning. I hope to answer them while traveling."

Lizzy pressed the letters against her chest, clearly not ready to give them up. "Gloria arrived. She's loading your luggage and the box of magazines now and needed a few minutes to reorganize her van. Did you verify your reservations for tonight?"

"Yes, my dear aunt. You trained me well."

Lizzy held out the small bundle of letters. "If these were business related, you'd have kept up with them."

Beth loved her aunt like a sister and usually got along with her, but clearly they needed a break from each other. For the last six months, it had felt like they were two old maids bickering back and forth. Lizzy was sure she knew how to direct Beth's life, and Beth was sure she didn't.

Beth simply nodded as she took the letters. Some were from relatives who lived outside Apple Ridge, and some were from friends she'd met over the years during her annual or semiannual buying-selling trips.

With the rest of her paperwork inside her black canvas satchel, she looped her arm through Lizzy's and led her through the aisles, around customers, and to the door of the shop.

When they stepped onto the porch, Lizzy wrapped one arm around Beth's waist. "You'll be careful, right?"

Beth pulled her into a hug, holding her for a long spell. "You drive me nuts, but I do believe I love you more than any niece has ever loved an aunt."

Lizzy took a deep breath that spoke of tears. "Are you sure you're up to this trip?" She put a bit of space between them. "It's hard to be away from family that long, and you'll spend more time with Englischers than with Amish."

"Months of planning and you ask me this now?"

In spite of August's heat, Lizzy's hands felt cool against her cheeks. "It's your first time to go since Henry…"

Why did her aunt insist on stating the obvious? "I know that. I'm fine. I'll always be fine, if for no other reason than to keep you from taking over my life and trying to run it for me. Do we need to tattoo the words 'Beth's fine' on the back of your hand?"

"A tattoo?" The male voice behind Beth was clearly that of Omar, their bishop.

She turned to see his smiling face. His gruff-sounding question didn't hide the amusement reflected in his eyes. Lizzy's face flushed a bit as she straightened her apron. Beth swallowed, never quite sure if he was teasing or nicely sharing his opinion.

His eyes stayed on her aunt for several long seconds, giving Beth a few moments to find her voice. "Uh…well…"

The bishop laughed. "It isn't a completely bad idea if it would get *somebody* we know to stop worrying so much." His eyes and smile moved to Beth. "But I think it will take more than the ink in a tattoo to do that." He gestured toward the van. "It looks like you're about ready to leave."

His sincere smile should warm her. It used to. But now whenever she was around Omar, her guilt pressed in heaviest of all—maybe because as bishop he might see into her, or maybe because he was Henry's uncle. Sometimes she was sure he knew her secret.

The bishop leaned against the porch column. "Your Daed says you'll be gone for three weeks, give or take a few days."

Wishing she knew what to do with her hands, she folded her arms and nodded. At least today if he shook her hand, the sweltering heat provided a good excuse for her sweaty palms. "Yes. It'll be a tight schedule, but I hope to get it all done."

The bishop studied her. "I'm sure you will. You always have."

She forced a smile, sickened at how she hid behind a facial expression. "Denki."

Gloria shut the doors to the back of the van. "I meant to get ice for the drinks Beth asked me to pack. Lizzy, can I get some from your house?"

"Sure, I'll give you a hand."

Gloria grabbed the cooler out of the backseat, and the two women hurried across the road to Lizzy's place. The bishop lifted the weight of Beth's satchel off her shoulder, and she released it. He went down the steps, and she had no choice but to follow him.

Her insides trembled, but she reminded herself that no Amish knew her truth. Not even the bishop. And unless Henry returned from the grave to tell, none ever would.

Omar stopped under the shade of the walnut tree. "Those of us who knew Henry miss him, but we're doing better."

No one really knew Henry.

Hoping to keep the conversation as light and breezy as possible, she kept her response brief and hoped he took the hint. "I know. I am too."

"Lizzy tells me otherwise."

She shifted, wishing Lizzy would believe her and stop talking to Omar about it. Her throat tightened. "You know, if you keep this up, we'll need a tattoo for you as well. It'll say, 'Beth's fine!' "

The man chuckled. "Okay, you're fine." He straightened. "Just don't bring back any forbidden items this trip. We've gone that route twice already, and I'd rather not repeat it, okay?"

"Ya, I know."

That was eight years ago. Did he still see her as a teenager? At the time it'd seemed harmless to purchase enlarged photos and canvas paintings Englischers had made of the Amish. Beth had defended her decision by telling Omar she'd hired Amish to make the frames for the items, no Amish person's face could be seen in any of the settings, they hadn't posed for any of the pictures, and the items were a sought-after commodity by their Englischer customers. Omar felt that snapping photos as the Amish went about their quiet lives was an unwelcome intrusion and that her allowing such photographs to become a part of her business only encouraged Englischers to be bolder with their cameras. He said if she'd told the frame builders what she planned to do with their work, they wouldn't have participated. She hadn't agreed, but he had final say, and she ended up keeping the frames and burning the artwork. She still bought frames regularly and filled them with nature scenes an Amish woman painted for her. Omar was a bit uncomfortable with nature scenes being sold for Englischers to hang on their walls and admire—as if they might fawn over them to the point of worship—but he allowed her to carry the items in the store. The man's heart was in the right place—she believed that completely—but his ways were more conservative than a lot of bishops'. At times she wondered what life in Apple Ridge would be like if he hadn't been chosen to be the bishop.

Lizzy and Gloria came out of her aunt's house and crossed the street. With the cooler in hand, Gloria headed for the van. "You ready?"

"Ya."

Hoping she'd return home with stacks of orders for Amish goods, she looked forward to what this time could accomplish. It'd been a while since she and Gloria had been gone overnight on business, but through the years, traveling with Gloria made for relaxed and enjoyable trips. Her shoulder-length gray hair always stayed pulled back in a loose bun, and her jean skirts with knit tops never changed with the Englischer styles. She seemed as comfortable wearing the same look year in and year out as the Amish were.

Beth hugged Lizzy. "I'll call you in a few days." As she walked toward the vehicle, the bishop walked beside her.

"Oh, wait. I almost forgot." Lizzy ran into the store, and Omar and Beth stopped.

Omar smiled. "Maybe you should just take her with you."

"Uh, maybe not."

A look of amusement and understanding flickered through his eyes. Fresh longing to confide her secret rippled through her, but hoping for that kind of friend was as childish as young Englischers wanting a fairy to bring money for a useless tooth.

The silence stretched between them, and Beth wrestled with her guilt. The store's screen door banged against its frame, ending the fight.

"I made your favorite spice cake." Lizzy placed the tin carrier in Beth's hands, gave her a quick hug, and opened the van door for her.

Three

The edges of papers fluttered wildly as wind whipped through the open windows of the van. Securing the order forms on her traveling desk, Beth continued working between stops. Nearly two weeks of traveling were behind them, and despite her weariness she had more orders than she'd hoped for.

"I'm not sure where that detour was supposed to reconnect us to the highway, but we're in the backwoods now." Gloria's voice barely registered over Beth's thoughts.

She finished jotting down the information that danced in her head and then glanced up. The view of the Ohio River had disappeared, and hills with thick trees rose on each side of them. "Are we north of Steubenville?"

"That much I'm sure of."

"How far back did you begin following a detour sign?"

"Ten miles."

"How far since you saw the last detour arrow?"

"Eight miles."

Beth laughed. "I think you definitely missed something. Let's just backtrack until we pick up that detour sign."

Gloria pressed the brake and steered the vehicle completely off the road and onto the shoulder. "I'll make a U-turn after the cars behind me pass. Sorry about this."

"No apologizing, Gloria. You do a great job." Studying the road ahead, Beth suppressed a yawn. Before a bend in the road, there stood a post with eight wooden signs hanging from it, each one bearing a different store's name. "I think there's a small town ahead."

Watching the rearview mirror, Gloria frowned. "You actually *want* to venture off the planned route?"

"Well, since we already have, and I really could stand to stretch my legs, we might as well look around a bit. We have almost an hour before we need to be at All That's Amish. Besides, maybe someone can tell us a better way to get there from here. We should only be ten or fifteen miles away."

"Okay." Gloria turned on the blinker and merged back onto the road.

Once they were closer to the town, they passed a sign that read Welcome to Tracing.

As soon as they rounded the bend, Beth's heart rate increased. "Gloria," she whispered, "look at this place."

The town had character, like something out of the eighteenth century—two-story clapboard stores side by side, a narrow main road separating the two rows of buildings. There was a hitching post with a horse and buggy tied to it. Wherever Tracing was in relation to Steubenville, Amish lived nearby.

They pulled into a gravel parking lot beside one of the stores.

As they got out of the vehicle, Beth spotted a hand-painted sign that read "Pete's Antiques two blocks ahead." An arrow pointed up a side street. For the first time in more than a year, intrigue ran through her.

Gloria stepped onto the sidewalk. "There's a café. How about a hot lunch? I'm sure we can get good directions there."

Searching for Pete's store, Beth walked several feet one way and then the other. Up a side street and on a small hill stood a cedar-sided building. A feeling she thought had died with Henry stirred within her. "There." Beth pointed. "I'll be in that store when you're finished. We can't take much time, or we'll be late for the next appointment."

"I'll bring the van around to get you. Can I bring you a sandwich?"

"Sure. You know I'm not picky."

"Well, not about food or getting lost, but you're tough on what's worthy to carry in the shops. Otherwise the van would be filled with samples for the display room by now."

"Ya, but I've taken a lot of orders, and Pete may be another one willing to buy."

Gloria laughed and headed for the café. Beth opened the van's door, stuffed the order forms into her satchel, and tucked it under her arm. She hurried across the street. The hill seemed to grow longer and steeper as she went.

Out of breath, she pushed herself to keep her speed as she mounted the wooden steps. The screen door swung open, and a man came out.

"Whoa." He chuckled and pressed his back against the door, holding it open for her. "A woman on a mission."

Embarrassed she hadn't seen him in time to slow down and use her manners, she dipped her head. "Denki." She intended to be polite and keep moving, but when she glanced at his face, his golden brown eyes stopped her cold. Intrigue collided with unease, and she told herself to go into the store. Yet she simply stood. He was in his mid to late twenties, Amish, and clean-shaven, like all single Amish men.

And something about him had her mesmerized. Did she know him?

His pursed lips did not hide his smile or his amusement at her gaping.

Stop gawking and go inside, Beth!

She cleared her throat, lowered her eyes, and slipped past him. Disobeying the wisdom she'd gained about single men, she turned to see him again. His smile was gone, but his eyes lingered, taking her in as much as she took him in.

Had they met somewhere? Maybe on one of her trips through the Ohio Amish community? He seemed oddly familiar.

Moreover, he felt…

An image of Henry moved into her mind, and she came to herself. He remained at the doorway. "Can I help you?"

"No, I…I'm just here to look around."

"There's the main room, which you're in, and a few rooms off to the sides. There's also more upstairs, including seasonal items. Pete's in the back with a customer, but he'll be out in a bit."

"Denki." Horrified at how brazen she must appear, she made a beeline to the stairs.

Once out of his sight, she found her breath and her good sense again. She'd simply remain upstairs for a bit and hope he'd been in the process of leaving when she nearly ran him over. Rattled, she closed her eyes and tried to even out her breathing. She'd felt a spark of interest for a man once before. He'd been a stranger to her too, and nothing would ever cause her to let down her guard like that again. Ready to forget and focus on her job, she began looking around the shop.

Searching through each room, she spotted nothing outstanding. Pete carried mostly antique pieces, all ordinary, but she couldn't stop walking the aisles of the rooms again and again. Old and new mattresses were propped against the walls, along with bedsprings and slats. Arrays of floor lamps with Tiffany-style stained-glass lampshades were scattered throughout, some old and some quite new. An Amish-made twin bed sat in one room with the dresser and matching hope chest in a separate room. The store carried a variety of items, but if this was how the management organized things, the sales weren't what they could be.

While all the rooms were much the same, she kept returning to one specific room. What continued to draw her back to this area? There had to be something. Threading her way through the packed aisles, she looked behind the bulky furniture. Under a draped quilt between a bed and a hope chest, she spotted the edge of a striking piece of wood, maybe part of a buffet.

She eased the quilt up. Surprised at her find, she sank to her knees.

A carving. More intricate in detail than anything she'd ever seen.

Unlike ordinary artwork, it was made from a log and sat on the ground like a small upturned stump. It stood about a foot high and was a foot in diameter. On it the artisan had created an entire scene of

Amish children playing in the snow on a hillside. The artist hadn't used paint, but she could easily see the carefully fashioned snow. A man stood off to the side, leaning against an intricately carved tree. She ran her fingers over the work, the details of which she couldn't believe or even have imagined possible.

"You like it?" A man's voice echoed through the room, but she didn't look up and was barely able to make herself respond.

"It's amazing."

"The Old Man himself made that. He's been carving since he was five. I think he might just have the hang of it."

"I'd say so, yes. Why are you hiding it up here?"

"It's a Christmas scene. Nobody buys winter stuff in August."

"I think people would purchase this any time of the year."

"You gonna buy it?"

Beth looked up to see a man in his sixties standing in the doorway. "Do you have more than this one piece?"

"Not right now. He probably has more in his shop. Most of what he makes is smaller. He's really good at making canes and walking sticks. We sell a lot of those."

"And this 'old man' is a friend of yours?"

"Yep. Probably the best one I've ever had."

"Does he live around here?"

"Not close, not far. And I can't see how that should make a difference on whether you want to buy it."

She pulled a business card out of her satchel and rose. "I'm Elizabeth Hertzler. Call me Beth. I'd be interested in talking with him."

He scratched his head. "You own a store in Pennsylvania?"

"Yes, but I also supply Amish and Englischer stores with Amish products—from indoor and outdoor furniture to swing sets to picture frames." She passed him a catalog. "If you need it, I have a skilled Amish person who can make it."

"I doubt he'd agree to sell like that. He handpicks his pieces of wood and takes months to create them. He went down a gorge last winter to get this one. He and his brother used a rope, a draft horse, and a lot of determination to drag it out."

"And then you hide it under a blanket."

The man laughed. "I guess so. He hasn't ever complained. Still, I'm not sure how it got shifted to this spot. Since most of his work depicts winter scenes, they catch more attention in cold weather. I put them near the entry of the store at Christmastime, and they sell pretty well then."

"I'm not interested in selling this one, but I'm sure I can find stores that would carry his work and display it in good view year round."

"I thought you owned a store."

"I'm not sure my bishop would allow us to carry this type of work."

"His bishop lets him make it."

"Your friend is Amish?"

"Yeah."

"Maybe that'll help my position if I try to convince my bishop. Regardless, I want this one. How much?"

"Seeing how you like it so much, how about a hundred dollars?"

"A hundred dollars?"

"Too much?"

"Too little. Why would you undervalue his work?"

"It's art by a man no one knows. I get the best price I can." The man smiled. "But if you think you can do better, I'll give you his address."

"I'll take the info with me. Unless it's on my way, I won't have time to talk with him this trip. Does he have a phone?"

"Nope. His bishop is strict about phones. Why'd you ask where he lived if you're not planning to go see him?"

"It's just a natural question. If I'm hoping to do business with someone, it helps to have an idea of their vicinity. Just like before I leave, I'll get your store's phone number and street address."

"I'll jot down all the info you need." He grabbed the carving off the floor. "And I'll get my nephew to carry this out for you. I'm guessing you have a driver."

"She'll be here in a few minutes. In the meantime would you care to look through our catalog?"

"Don't waste any time, do ya?" Pete took the catalog and flipped through the pages.

No, she didn't like wasting time, but her heart and body had demanded she spend over a year grieving. Still, it seemed Lizzy had been right; she should have gotten out among people long before now. Who knows what detours she might have missed while on her road of isolation?

Four

*A*fter removing the entire window unit, Jonah straddled the sill. With one leg inside the schoolhouse and one outside it, he looked up from his work. A row of horseless carriages filled the front lawn of the school. Inside the pasture fence stood a dozen grazing horses, patiently waiting for their owners. Half a dozen workers on the roof hammered away. Under the massive oaks, women filled the picnic tables with breads, cheeses, and vegetables fresh from the gardens, and children played games, enjoying the last weeks of summer break.

The community worked on this old one-room schoolhouse each year before classes began. Sometimes Jonah wondered if it would be easier to build a new one, but anytime the subject came up, the Amish school board voted against it.

The nonstop hammering overhead drowned out the voices of the women and children. With a small claw bar in hand, Jonah removed each nail from the window and checked the soundness of the framing. His mind still lingered on the woman he'd seen at Pete's a few days ago.

Those deep blue eyes against black lashes had almost knocked him over, even with his cane to steady him. Her soft yet deep and confident voice still filled his head. It was embarrassing to give her a second thought, let alone *every* thought. She wore black, the color of a brokenhearted widow. She could have been grieving for a family member, but something about her said the pain she carried was different from that of losing a relative. He guessed she'd lost a large piece of herself. But the rest of her stirred him—as if she needed someone, a friend or relative, to help her sand away the pain etched into her life and dig deeper to carve a new scene.

He'd never considered sanding off someone's old life, not even when they'd lost a loved one. It seemed to him the past carvings should be preserved and a new spot found for fresh carvings. Or perhaps new carvings should include the old carvings. But to remove what had been and start fresh? He was mistaken about that. Had to be.

"Jonah." His grandmother spoke over the loud banging. She held out a cup of water.

He hadn't realized she'd come into the schoolroom. He wiped his brow. "Denki, *Mammi*." He took a long drink. "Even sitting in a window doesn't provide enough of a breeze in this heat."

"Only bad shepherds use entrances other than the door. Didn't your mother teach you anything?"

"Yes, she did. That you're a troublemaker." He tried to keep a straight face but wasn't able to hold back his laughter.

"How many window units will you need to replace?"

"All of them. The sashes are too rotten to make it through another school year, but so far all the casings have been completely sound."

"So you've been at this for a couple of days?"

"Ya."

"You met the new teacher and had help, then?"

He wasn't fooled. She knew he had plenty of help from the men in the community. Her curiosity centered on the new teacher.

"Yes to both, Mammi. Every man in our community has come to help as time allowed. Right now they're either helping the women with other things or on the roof repairing bad shingles."

"Your presence here has caused a fresh buzz among the young women." Mammi motioned out the window. "You need to find one who suits you before you're too old."

He finished drinking the water she'd brought him and passed her the cup. "If only one of them was half as amazing as you…"

Mammi moved closer. "Stop teasing your poor grandmother and find someone. I've seen you carve life out of deadwood. Can't you try to do that in a relationship?"

"A worthwhile relationship is like finding the right wood. When it's the right one, I'll know it."

"And by the time your idealism blends with realism, you may have missed your chance."

Using the claw bar, he pulled another nail out of the casing. "So, Mammi, why is there a bee in your prayer *Kapp* about this all of a sudden?"

"The new schoolteacher, Martha." She tapped him on the arm, and with her eyes she directed him to look outside near the picnic tables.

Martha passed half a sandwich to one of the children.

"While I was talking with her about the upcoming school year, she kept looking your way." His grandmother held out her hand for the claw bar. He didn't give it to her.

"Maybe she's never seen a carpenter with a bum leg and two missing fingers."

"Nonsense. She was drawn to you. I saw it in her eyes. Now go speak to her. At least give her a chance."

He removed another nail. "She's too young."

"Too young? She's probably twenty-two, and you're only twenty-eight."

"No." He placed several bent nails in his grandmother's open hand. "She's about seventeen, and I'm about forty, figuratively speaking."

"Well, sometimes older men connect well with younger women." She wrapped her frail hand around his wrist and pulled.

Giving in to her, he climbed out of the windowsill. If it'd make her feel better for him to speak to the woman, he could do that much. And while pleasing his grandmother, he'd get a bite to eat from the picnic tables.

She brushed bits of wood off his shirt. "At least talk with her a little before deciding she's not right for you. Tell her you have a question about how she wants something done in her classroom or you want to show her how the window works."

"I have no questions, and if she needs to be shown how a window works, we need a new teacher."

"Jonah Kinsinger, you're as stubborn as your grandfather."

"You know this, and yet you insist on shoving me into some poor woman's life."

She passed him his cane, turned him around, and nudged him forward. "Go. And find the beauty in whatever wood is in front of you."

As innocent as her words were meant to be, they carried a mild dishonor to him. Aside from a few pangs of loneliness once in a while, he was content being single. As the thought rumbled through him, the memory of the stranger in black stood before him again. She'd captivated some part of him, but it wasn't her beauty that had piqued his interest. Like an ancient oak, she carried hidden years, and as an artist, he was drawn to it.

He walked outside, and cold liquid splattered over his head and down his neck. "Whoa."

"Jonah." Mark's surprised voice came from above him.

Jonah looked up to see his friend on the roof with an upturned cup in his hand. A couple of men moved to Mark's side to see what had happened.

Jonah licked his lips. "Mmm. Lemonade."

Laughing, the men returned to work.

Martha brought him a dishtowel, looking more concerned than amused.

"Thanks." Jonah wiped his face. "You're standing in dangerous territory unless you prefer to wear your lemonade rather than drink it."

She motioned toward the picnic table. "Maybe you'd prefer trying on some food instead."

Her sense of humor amused him, which would make the chore his grandmother had laid before him easier.

Why was it so hard for married men and women to accept that he liked being single? Only one thought came to his mind—*they* needed to find a better hobby.

Five

Children's laughter echoed across the snow-covered hills. Beth shivered, watching from a distance. Her feet ached from the cold, and her fingers were numb. A little Amish boy got off his sled and faced her. A younger girl took him by the hand. They stood motionless, watching Beth.

She opened her mouth to speak, but no words came out. A man moved among the trees, calling to them. When they didn't come, he walked closer and called again. The children motioned for Beth to join them, but her legs worked no better than her mouth. As the man drew closer, he smiled and gestured toward the field where half a dozen other children played. Too cold to move, Beth began to recognize the children. She knew their names, didn't she? But from where?

The frigid air around her seemed too much to bear, but the man and the children appeared as warm as if they sat in front of a wood stove. As if reading her thoughts, the man tilted his head and opened his jacket, revealing heaps of embers glowing in his chest. The children followed suit, showing a bonfire inside their tiny upper bodies.

With stiff fingers Beth unhooked her black cape and looked at her heart. Anxiety spread through her body. Where they had embers and fire, she had frozen tundra.

The man touched his chest and then held out an ember for her. Embarrassed at her frozen soul, she wanted to hold out her hand, but she couldn't. Even if she could lift her arm, he stood too far away. She tried to walk toward him but couldn't move. He held out his hand again.

Her jaws fought against the wires that kept them clasped. "I...I can't."

He looked straight through her, and she understood that he couldn't come any closer. She had to be the one who moved. Snow began to fall, and the sky grew dark, but she couldn't budge an inch. The sadness in the children's eyes ran deeper than Beth could comprehend. They clasped hands and ran back to the others. The man stood, watching her. A tear slid down his face, and one by one the children faded into nothingness.

His eyes pleaded with her to find the strength to move forward and take the ember, but even as she willed herself to take a step, he too faded away.

Beth sat up in bed, trying to steady her pounding heart.

That dream—and a dozen others like it over the last two weeks—was as bad as the ones that had plagued her since Henry died. Nightmares of him clinging to her as rain poured from the skies and formed rivers that swept him away while she remained on solid ground, her clothing soaked as the temperatures dropped and freezing winds began to blow. The images were too close to reality, and she couldn't find freedom whether Henry was alive or dead, whether she was awake or asleep. Thoughts of Henry always brought confusion, but lately the dreams weren't about him.

Sliding into her housecoat, she moved to the wooden steps that led to the store below. The darkness inside the stairwell felt familiar and welcoming, and she sat down. As the reassurance of the place wrapped around her, she began to shake free of the dream.

She folded her arms and propped them on her knees, making a place to rest her head. While trying not to think about anything, sleep drifted over her again. A few moments later the sound of a horse neighing made her jerk awake. It took only a moment to realize the animal had been in her dream.

It was useless trying to sleep, whether on the stairway or in bed. Rising to her feet, she grabbed the handrail, feeling a bit dizzy. She might as well get a little work done.

Making her way down the stairs, through the store, and into her office, she couldn't help wondering when dreams started mixing with a sense of reality. After entering her office, she slid her hands across the paper-strewn desk top, searching for a set of matches. Her fingertips brushed against the carving she'd bought nearly two weeks ago. It took up a good bit of her desk, but she'd made room for it.

Forget the matches. Her mind was too cloudy to think anyway. She walked around her desk and sat in the chair. Gliding her fingertips over the intricate detail of the carving, she wished her aunt would at least go meet with the artist.

She'd lost the argument with the bishop that it wasn't an idol. He quoted the second commandment—"thou shalt not make unto thee any graven image." Because the wood had human images carved into it, Omar felt it was too close to what the Old Testament warned against. Since faceless dolls were commonplace among her people for the same reasoning, Beth had little grounds for appeal. His decision was final, but she held on to the hope that she could convince Englischer stores to carry the carvings. That wasn't working either since Lizzy refused to let her try. She said it would disrespect their bishop. Beth's Daed and uncles sided with Lizzy, so for now Beth could do nothing.

If her aunt was willing to talk with the artist and his bishop, she might feel differently. Then Beth could at least sell the man's work to Englischer stores. But Lizzy seemed more interested in pleasing Bishop Omar than in making a difference in an artist's life.

Beth sighed, wishing they could see the carvings like she did, as no more of an idol than an Amish-sewn wall hanging. Maybe then the strange dreams where the children and the man from the carving beckoned her to enter their snowy Amish world would disappear.

Standing on the porch of the store, Lizzy slid her key into the lock and turned it. Inside, she noticed the door to the steps that led to Beth's bedroom stood open. Lizzy moved to the foot of the stairwell. "Beth?"

She heard no movement upstairs. Turning slowly in a circle, she expected her niece's head to pop up from between the aisles. Usually by this time each morning, the two of them had shared a breakfast, talked business, and begun preparing to open the place at nine. "Beth?"

Her heart ran wild, and panic over her niece sliced through her. The young woman hadn't been herself in so long. She handled herself well, but Lizzy knew something ate at her. Suddenly Lizzy admitted to herself that images of Beth taking her own life slipped into her mind at times.

"Beth!"

When she didn't respond, Lizzy rushed to the office and pushed against the slightly open door. Her niece was slouched over the desk, her fingers resting on that carving she'd bought.

Her legs shaking, Lizzy touched her niece's face. "Honey?"

Beth moaned and drew a sleepy breath. Unable to remain standing, Lizzy eased into a chair next to the desk.

Blinking, Beth frowned and lifted her head. "Good morning." Her voice sounded hoarse and groggy.

"Did you sleep here all night?"

Beth took a deep breath and rubbed her eyes. "No." Stretching her neck, she yawned. "I didn't sleep much anywhere. What time is it?"

"A little after eight."

Beth looked straight at her and narrowed her eyes. "Is something wrong?"

Unable to share her fears, Lizzy shook her head. Beth came around to the front of the desk. She didn't look depressed, so why did Lizzy's imagination get the best of her? As soon as the question ran through her mind, she knew the answer. Her niece had changed, and Lizzy feared she might be getting worse rather than better.

Beth brushed her fingertips across Lizzy's forehead. "Then why is there fear in your eyes?"

"I…I couldn't find you."

Beth sat on the edge of the desk. "So you thought mountain lions came out of the hills, into the shop, and ate me?"

"My imagination got away with me, and I…" Lizzy swallowed hard, willing herself to say what was on her heart. "You worry me. It's like you're not the same person anymore."

Beth patted her hand. "I know."

Does she really know how much she's changed? And how completely scared and out of control Lizzy felt concerning her?

"Why are you sleeping in the office?"

Her niece's delicate hands caressed the carving. "It calls to me. Dreams that make little sense fade in and out as if they're trying to tell me something." She raised one eyebrow and mockingly pointed a finger at Lizzy. "And you know how I feel about people talking to me when I'm trying to sleep."

In spite of her humor about it, her niece's blue eyes held absolute rawness, as if Henry had died yesterday rather than sixteen months ago. And Beth had asked only one thing of Lizzy since Henry had died. Just one.

"I've decided to go see this artist of yours."

Beth's eyes grew large, and a beautiful smile seemed to remove some of her paleness. "Really?"

"Ya."

A spark of delight stole through the usual sadness in Beth's eyes, and Lizzy's heart expanded with hope. Maybe her niece would find her way back to herself yet.

"I'll call Gloria and set up a trip," Lizzy said. "I'm not making any promises, though. I'm checking it out. That's it."

"Then you'll meet the carver. And I bet you'll be glad you did."

"Maybe."

Or maybe Beth was hunting for fulfillment outside the Old Ways and Lizzy was helping her.

Six

As Gloria drove down the back roads to Jonah Kinsinger's place, Lizzy prayed. Her niece had no idea how awkward this upcoming cold call might be. She didn't want to build up the artist's hopes, yet she needed to talk to him about Beth's possibly selling his work to Englischer tourist shops.

Beth was so much better with this kind of stuff, but if she were here, she might pursue the work without regard to the bishop's opinion.

Gloria slowed the vehicle and turned into a gravel driveway. "According to our directions and the mailboxes, this should be it."

From the looks of it, two homes, maybe three, used this triple-wide driveway and turnaround. According to the mailboxes, two of the places belonged to men named Jonah Kinsinger.

"Which one?" Gloria asked.

"Let's stop at this first one. It looks like the original homestead, and the Jonah Kinsinger we're looking for is an older man, according to Beth."

Gloria put the van in Park. Lizzy opened the door, viewing the house. "I shouldn't be more than twenty minutes if this is the right house."

Gloria held up a paperback. "I'll pull under a shade tree and enjoy my time."

Lizzy went up the porch steps, knocked, and waited. Through the screen she could see a woman, about seventy years old, hurrying to the door. Beyond her, two young girls tried to catch sunshine in their aprons. She remembered playing that game as a little girl. It had never held much interest for Beth. If it couldn't be scrubbed or organized, her niece never cared about it, even as a toddler.

The woman smiled as she opened the door. "Can I help you?"

"Hi, I'm Elizabeth Hertzler. I own an Amish dry goods store in Pennsylvania, and I'm looking for Jonah Kinsinger, the carver."

"He and his brother are working at the lumberyard." She glanced at the clock. "But they should be in for lunch within the hour if you care to wait."

"He lives here, then?"

"No, but he'll eat lunch here today."

"I came to talk about his carvings and hopefully see more of his work."

"You're welcome to go into his shop and look around." She stepped onto the porch and pointed several hundred feet away. "The door is at the far end."

"Thank you."

Lizzy went to the van and spoke through the open window. "He's supposed to be back within the hour. If I leave, I could miss him."

"Then wait," Gloria said.

"Do you want to come with me?"

"I'd rather read, if you don't mind."

"Okay."

With sweat running down her back, Lizzy walked to the shop. September had arrived, but summer's heat remained strong. She knocked on the solid door and then tried the knob. The door opened, and she walked in. The room glowed with a golden hue. Unfinished, honey-colored paneling covered the four walls, and sunlight poured in through several windows. A blue tarp hung in a doorway, blocking her view into the next room. What appeared to be a handmade box sat on the table.

Thinking she heard children whispering, Lizzy moved to the window and raised the shade. She expected to see the girls who had been inside the main house, but she saw no one. The voices grew clearer, as if they'd come into the shop with her.

She walked to the hanging blue tarp and pulled it to the side. The adjoining room looked like an old outbuilding—dirt floors, stalls where calves might have once been kept, and shelves filled with pieces of wood, paint cans, and cardboard boxes.

"Hello?"

Silence filled the room. Moving deeper into the building, she thought she heard a child giggle.

"Hello?"

Not minding a quick game of hide-and-seek, she continued walking until she stood at the back of the long, narrow building. There were no windows, but a few rays of sunlight streamed through the cracks in the wooden walls. Through the hazy gray air, she noticed an old, damaged sleigh.

"Is someone in here?"

Seeing no one, she worked her way around the sleigh, moving slowly so she didn't stumble. On the far side of the sleigh, she knelt, looking under it for signs of the children.

A cane and two black boots came into sight. The footwear shifted.

Embarrassed and addled, she stood.

A silhouette of a man passed her an unlit candle. He struck a match, revealing that, in spite of the cane, he was in his twenties. After lighting the wick he shook the match and tossed it into the dirt. "Can I help you with something?" His voice sounded warm, but he looked uncertain of her.

"I…I'm Elizabeth Hertzler." She brushed dirt off her apron. "I… thought I heard children in here playing. I shouldn't have searched for them this far back into your shop, but it's just…I got caught up in following the sounds of their whispers…" She wiped her hands down the sides of her dress. "From the look on your face, I may never redeem myself."

He gestured for her to follow him. "You'll feel better once I show you something."

They wound through a darker section of the building, making her glad he'd brought a candle. A moment later he popped open a rickety door. The wind blew the candle out, and the sounds she'd heard earlier echoed through the bright sunshine.

She blinked, waiting for her eyes to adjust to the light. The young man placed his hand under her forearm. "Watch your step."

Glancing around as her eyes focused, she expected the fierce white view to retreat and reveal children. Instead, she saw a terrace of some sort. From the eaves of a gazebo hung at least two dozen hand-carved wind chimes.

She stepped closer, awed at the find. "They sound like children whispering and laughing. How is that possible?"

"They're designed to make inviting tones. I've found that what a person hears tends to vary." His brown eyes held no pity concerning her intelligence and no judgment against her behavior. Whoever he was, she was glad he'd been the one to discover her on her knees beside a broken sleigh and not someone more critical.

"Does this Jonah Kinsinger make these too?"

"I do."

Startled, she tried not to look too surprised. "You do?"

He nodded.

"And the large carving from Pete's—you did that too?"

"Yes. Pete said that you liked it and that he gave you my address."

Her conscience pricked when he mistook her for Beth, but something told her not to correct him. The business cards and catalogs they passed out had the store's name and phone number and the name Elizabeth Hertzler. It wasn't the Amish way to promote an individual, so if people knew how to reach "Elizabeth" at the store, that was all they needed to know.

"But I don't understand. I thought you would be old."

"Probably because Pete's called me Old Man since I was five, when he began teaching me how to whittle."

Her nerves were still on edge, and she tried to gather herself. "Your bishop allows you to sell your carvings, including the wind chimes?"

He motioned to a set of chairs under the shade of the gazebo. "You look a bit pale. Would you like to sit for a spell?"

"Very much. Denki."

"Can I get you a glass of water? My place is just beyond those trees."

"No. I'm fine." As she said the word *fine* to describe herself, visions of her beautiful, lonely niece entered her mind. She took a seat. "So your bishop doesn't feel that you're creating graven images?"

"Well, he might have had a few reservations. You'd need to talk to him about that. Over the years I've wondered if his decision was based on favoritism."

As the eeriness from earlier began to fade, she saw a depth in his eyes that drew her like his work had drawn her niece. "Favoritism?"

"When I was injured at fifteen, I couldn't get around well enough to do an apprenticeship, so he allowed me to do something I'd had the ability for since I was young." Jonah shrugged, and a mischievous smile seemed to come out of hiding. "The bishop's my Daed."

"Oh." She studied the intricate details of the wind chimes. "I'm afraid that's not much help to me. I've thought about carrying your work in my store, but your father allowing you isn't likely to convince my bishop."

"I'm not really interested in creating pieces on demand to sell, anyway."

"Not interested? Your work is gorgeous, and it touched the very soul of…" A thought swept through her, scattering pieces of a plan across her like sawdust caught in the wind.

Beth.

Jonah's work stirred her. Called to her. Wakened her. But whatever else it did, it refused to be ignored. Beth could ignore her own needs, her own heart, and forge ahead with life, but she hadn't tuned out the artistry of Jonah Kinsinger.

As she looked at this young man, knowing Beth felt a connection, the plan unrolled inside her.

She stared into his eyes, hoping what she was about to do was the right thing. "Giving it up for a girl, are you?"

Jonah laughed. "I never said I was giving it up." Using his thumb, he pushed his straw hat back a little. The gesture revealed two missing fingers, probably more damage sustained in the accident. "It's not about money."

"I'm sure it's not." Lizzy moved to the edge of the gazebo. The place was an odd mixture—a rather dilapidated building attached to a much newer shop. A beautiful garden area with an expensive gazebo behind the old place. To her left, a recently built cabin almost hidden behind a grove of ancient trees.

And a handsome young man with a skill that calls to my niece.

"Your carving seems to carry life in it."

Somber as a church meeting, he gazed at her. "The piece you wish to sell in your store was a royal pain from the get-go. The tree lay at the bottom of a gorge, and I tried to ignore it for months. But by last winter I couldn't disregard it any longer, so I wrestled it out with my brother's help and took it to my shop." He leaned back against the railing. "And the truth is, I was glad to be done with it. Just as soon not have that experience again. So if you're looking for a carver, I'm probably not your man."

"Is that why there's a layer of dust on your tools and the wood on your workbench?"

"The only thing I made out of that tree was the carving you bought. I cut other pieces with the intention of carving scenes in each, but…it's just not in me. Still, I guess I'd be pleased to sell or put on consignment whatever is in my shop that I've made from other trees."

"This isn't what I expected when I came here. You're supposed to be excited and trying to convince me to get permission to carry these items."

He smiled and cradled one chime in the palm of his hand. "When I was injured, if my Daed hadn't given me freedom to carve, I'm not sure I could have stood it. I was stuck in a wheelchair for nearly a year. Lost all sense of who I'd thought I was. Surgeries and physical therapy were constant and painful. And as selfish as it sounds now, being without two fingers felt totally humiliating, like God had singled me out to mock. My Daed gave me a way to transfer my emotions into a lump of wood." He released the chime, making lovely tones float through the air.

Wishing Beth could hear this man's understanding of life after loss, Lizzy's plan became clearer to her. "I've never married, so I don't have children, but I do have someone I love as if she were my own. And right now she's in that bad place you spoke of. But it's been nearly a year and a half since her loss, and I don't know why it continues to be so heavy."

"Maybe for you it wouldn't be, but for her it is."

A dinner bell clanged loudly.

He motioned to the steps of the gazebo. "Come eat with us, Elizabeth. It's our family's once-a-month workweek gathering. You can meet all sorts of Kinsingers and three other Jonahs. Afterward, I'll load you up with the carvings I do have."

When he spoke her full name instead of her nickname, Lizzy knew the door to her hope stood wide open. As they walked around the side of the building, she saw Gloria waiting for her. "I can't stay." She stared into the crystal blue sky. Part of her felt as if she was about to follow God's leading, and part of her felt like a manipulative woman.

Hoping her plan didn't push Beth further from her, she dared to give her idea a try. "Jonah, meeting you today has been the best treat I've had in a long time. I'm hoping you'd be willing to keep in touch with me by mail."

The way he looked at her, she knew he thought she was a bit off-center. Still, he nodded. "I suppose that'd be fine."

"Good." She stopped at the foot of the steps that led to what had to be his grandmother's place. "Did Pete give you my card, or do I need to get one for you?"

"He passed it to me."

"Even though it says Elizabeth Hertzler, you should write to Beth. I mean…" She tried to word it so she wasn't actually lying. "Beth, Lizzy, Elizabeth—they're all forms of my name."

He raised both eyebrows, looking more skeptical. "Beth." He lightly spoke the name without relaying either question or statement in his tone. "Pete did say you went by Beth."

Her throat seemed to close, but she pressed on anyway, hoping Pete hadn't said anything about Beth's age. "And you shouldn't feel obligated to write that it was good to meet me. I mean, we can say that right now and skip the fluff in the letters. Don't you think?"

Lines deepened as he looked at her much like he had when he'd found her by the broken sleigh.

"Jonah." A tall, gray-haired man stepped onto the porch, and relief that she could stop stammering flooded her. "Will your guests be staying for lunch? We have plenty."

Jonah looked at her. "You're welcome to stay."

"I really need to load up some of your carvings so I can be on my way. Hopefully, I'll be able to talk Omar into letting us carry them in our dry goods store."

Jonah nodded and turned to the man on the porch. "*Daadi,* this is Elizabeth Hertzler from Apple Ridge, Pennsylvania. She owns a store there. Elizabeth…Beth, this is my grandfather, Jonah Kinsinger."

The man descended the steps. "Apple Ridge?" He said the name thoughtfully, and she realized he was trying to think of any Amish he might know from the area. She wanted to avoid that conversation before her letter-writing plan was ruined.

"It's so good to meet you. Your grandson has quite a skill for carving."

The older Jonah smiled broadly. "Can't say he's ever set his hand to anything he didn't become remarkable at."

Jonah smiled. "The favoritism thing I mentioned earlier? Uh, it runs in the family."

Lizzy chuckled. "I really do need to get going."

"Ya, Pete said you kept to a schedule." He turned to his grand-father. "Tell Mammi I'll be in shortly. I need to help Beth load up a few carvings."

Her plan was destined to fail. She knew that. But if it worked for a week or two, that might be enough time for Jonah and his wisdom about loss and dealing with it to reach inside Beth and make a difference. That was what Lizzy wanted most of all—and she was willing to suffer Beth's anger over it.

And if Beth were ever free from all that held her heart captive, she might actually see the man who was standing here.

Seven

The clip-clop of a horse and buggy on the road filtered through the open window of Beth's office. She'd moved the wringer washer outside that morning so she could both wash and hang the laundry before being stuck in this tiny room all day. Now she sat at her desk, shuffling endless amounts of paperwork. Buying-and-selling trips were much more fun than this, but since so many Amish could no longer make a living farming, many depended on her to sell their handcrafted products. She loved being a source of help for her people, but it required her to be behind this desk a lot.

Sitting back, she studied the details of the carving. For the tenth time that hour, she ran her fingers over the tracery. How could anyone make such intricate cuts into a block of wood?

When someone knocked on the door, she came to herself and returned her focus to her work. *"Kumm rei."*

Her aunt opened the door, holding up a stack of letters.

"Denki." Beth pointed to a tray on her desk.

Lizzy placed them in the holder. "Jonah Kinsinger wrote a letter." She took the top envelope off the stack and held it out.

"For me?" Beth stared at the envelope. The bishop hadn't budged on giving them permission. "He's probably wondering what Omar has decided. I don't know what to say to him. I can't do anything to help him sell his work. I did my best to convince Omar. You even gave it some effort."

"I didn't just give it *some* effort." Lizzy pointed the letter at her, wagging it as if it were her index finger. "I went to see Jonah as you asked. I brought some of his work back. And then I showed the pieces to Omar and talked to him about it, just the same as you did."

"I tried to convince him. You straddled the fence."

"He's our head, the top church leader over several districts. Is it our place to try to change his mind and heart? Shouldn't that be left in God's hands? We presented our request, and he doesn't feel he can allow such a thing, at least not yet."

"Omar closed the door, so that's the end of it? It's over?"

"He's a good man, Beth. Always has been. I believe if we're all praying, God will side with whoever's right, and Omar is the kind of person who will hear Him. Now rest in that, and answer Jonah."

"I don't have anything but bad news to share with Jonah."

"That's ridiculous. At what point did you become so negative? You have friendship to offer along with your love of his work. I'd say that's not *all* bad news." Lizzy held the envelope out to her again.

Looking at her aunt's face, she couldn't help but smile. "Denki."

"Gern Gschehne."

Laughing at the sassy way Lizzy chose to tell her she was welcome, Beth watched as she closed the door.

Maybe her aunt was right. She did have friendship to offer. And maybe the old man just needed a friend.

She slid her finger under the seal and realized it was already open. Either it had never been closed properly, or her aunt had already read it. Although either of them opened whatever store mail came in, it wasn't like Lizzy to open Beth's personal mail. But, after all, Jonah Kinsinger was a business relationship.

After pulling out the letter and unfolding it, Beth wondered if he'd written the letter himself or if he'd dictated it to someone, because the printing seemed awfully neat for an elderly man. Then again, each word seemed as perfectly chiseled as his woodwork.

Beth,

It's been encouraging to know that my carving caught your eye and that you hope to sell it in your shop. It's been quite a while since anyone showed this kind of interest.

Maybe that's why I'm not really interested in carving for money, or maybe it's because that one work about wore me out.

I spotted the log a little less than two years ago while riding bareback through the woods. That's a great pastime of mine. I like getting out by myself. Sometimes I pack a tent and a bit of food and meander hundreds of acres for days before returning home.

The moment I saw that fallen tree, even at a distance, it burned into my memory. But it lay in a gorge with no easy way to get it out. The land belonged to a widow woman Pete knows. She doesn't allow cutting of timber on her land, even when it's a fallen tree.

Well, you can imagine that I'd have much rather left it there than try to pull an entire tree up the side of an overgrown crag. So I left it.

But as the months passed, I couldn't get the richness of that particular tree or the possible carvings that could be made from it out of my mind.

I visited the widow and asked if I could cut the log into sections, but her husband never wanted anything cut from that forest area, and she had to honor that.

For a second time, I decided to leave it, but as you can tell from the piece you found at Pete's, dead wood has a stronger will than I do.

So with my cane in hand and a rope over my shoulder, I descended into the canyon in hopes of being mightier in muscle than I am in will.

It wasn't to be—not that I actually thought it would. But some things in life are just that way. They demand more of you than you have, and even

KNOWING YOU'LL LOSE, YOU HAVE TO ATTEMPT IT ANYWAY.

OR IS THAT JUST ME?

WELL, I NEED TO GO BEFORE SUPPER CATCHES
FIRE. . . AGAIN.

JONAH

Beth paused, soaking up his humor and openness. The carving hadn't caught her eye, as he'd said. It had snagged her heart. She should tell him that. He hadn't told her how he got that log out of the forest. How odd to bargain with an old woman who would let him have the felled tree but wouldn't let him cut it while it remained on her property. And Beth had to set him straight about the piece she'd brought home—she didn't intend to sell it.

She read his letter again.

In spite of the freezing winds that continually circulated inside her, warmth spread across her chest. Her hidden guilt had isolated her in ways she'd never imagined possible, but the letter eased her loneliness a little, and she felt something besides regret and her sense of duty to those around her. Was it possible every hidden part of who she'd once been—her heart, passion, and ability to connect—had not been fully destroyed after all?

Then a memory returned, and she saw herself on bended knee in the pouring rain.

For her part in Henry's death, she should be too numb to want a new friendship. Her relationship with Henry had shown her things she hadn't known about herself. She wasn't good at loyalty, yet she knew without it friendship was simply heartache waiting to happen. If she were capable of true devotion, Henry would be alive. When he died, she'd vowed to remain single forever.

But Jonah was old, and he would never need to test her endurance for commitment. She trusted that as an Amish man, he had plenty of family and friends who possessed strengths he could rely on. Surely even she could give what little he was asking for.

She opened a drawer and pulled out her best stationery.

Eight

On his back porch Jonah sipped a cup of coffee, watching as the first rays of daylight illuminated the canopy of leaves on the massive oaks. The deep greens of summer foliage carried the first hints of changing to gold, yellow, and red. Each year the sight begged him to watch endlessly. The colors of summer slowly faded, allowing the true color of the leaf to shine through. And then one day he'd wake to find their color had grown no brighter, and soon the radiant golds, reds, and yellows would tinge with brown, bringing with it a different type of beauty.

The front door slammed, and someone stomped through his home like a horse, vibrating the house. Jonah angled his head toward his left shoulder. "Coffee's on the stove."

"I have a wife who makes mine, and she does a right good job." His brother walked through the french doors and onto the porch with a cup of Jonah's steaming coffee. "But I thought I'd make sure yours weren't poison."

"Ya, just in case I rise early every day to brew toxins for myself."

Amos sipped the drink and made a face. "Broken buggy wheels, I think it might be dangerous to drink this stuff."

He took a seat in the rocker, and it moaned under the weight of him. At six foot seven inches, his brother was one of the largest men Jonah had ever known. He had the hands of a giant and a heart to match.

"I don't get it." Amos motioned toward the field. "It's a bunch of trees with leaves."

Jonah laughed. "And yet you join me and insult my coffee nearly every morning." Mist rose from the bottom land along the foot of the mountain until the top edge of the fog disappeared into the surrounding air as if it'd never existed. The early morning sun would soon burn off the remaining vapor. In spite of the birds chanting loudly, the morning seemed to hold on to a peaceful quietness.

Amos finished drinking most of his coffee before tossing the drips off the porch. "My gut can't take too much of that stuff." He placed his hands on the arms of the rocker and pushed himself up. "We got work to do. Oh, wait." He dug into his pants pocket. "Speaking of my wife, she checked your mailbox yesterday."

Jonah took the letter.

"It's from a girl." Amos's teasing grin didn't hide the seriousness in his eyes.

Jonah read the return address. "No, it's from Elizabeth Hertzler. You saw her in my driveway about a month ago."

"She was a nice-looking woman but a little older than I'd hoped you'd find."

His brother had shared his opinion for two reasons—to voice his concern and to let Jonah know he supported whatever he wanted. "Go gather eggs for Mammi and Daadi while I read my letter."

Amos left, whistling as he tromped through the house. Jonah ripped open the top of the envelope and pulled out the parchment-looking paper.

Dear Jonah,

It was so nice to receive your letter. It's been a very long time since I enjoyed anything as much as I enjoyed reading about your life. I can understand the desire to camp out in the forest—although I'll admit the idea of sleeping in a tent sounds dreadful, and a forest has too many creepy-crawlies for my taste.

Jonah laughed out loud, and the wind running through the leaves made it seem like the oaks joined him. Her truthfulness by itself kept him chuckling. He hoped Beth could see the majesty of the great outdoors. He refocused on the letter.

It's past midnight as I sit alone in my office. The minutes began ticking by hours ago, and I continue to wrestle with what to share and what to keep to myself. Your carving sits on my desk, and the smoky flame from my grandmother's kerosene lamp casts its glow over your artwork, causing the faces to change as the fire burns unsteadily. And the longer I sit here, the more I want to write what I'm thinking.

I'm glad you shared with me about finding the piece of wood and how you fought with whether to drag it out of the gorge or not. Your carving did not catch my eye as much as it snagged my heart. That log would not let you forget it, and your carving does much the same to me.

I must dare to be boldly open, so I can tell you that your work causes me to dream. Parts of the dreams are disturbing, but I'd forgotten what it feels like to be stirred by life.

I find it a little troubling to think a lifeless object can awaken one's soul, but your work has done that for me. I feel hope once again, and although I don't deserve it, I'm grateful for it. From the moment I saw this piece at Pete's, I never intended to sell it.

You didn't tell me how you got the tree out of the canyon and back to your shop.

Looking forward to hearing from you again,
Beth

"Jonah!" Amos hollered. "Daylight's burning."

Jonah folded the letter and shoved it and the envelope into his pocket. Beth's voice on paper didn't sound like she had in person. When here, she seemed nervous and scattered, but on paper she sounded serene and centered. After he finished at the sawmill for the day, he'd write to her again.

He set his mug on the railing, grabbed his cane, and walked around the side of the house. Her letter was an odd mix of thoughts and emotions. Even in its brevity it conveyed business, open admiration of his work, and hesitation to share the rawness she felt inside. Maybe that was why she sounded so different in her letter than at the farm.

He'd heard quite a few things inside that note, although he couldn't identify them. As the day wore on and he cut fresh lumber and sold from the seasoned stacks, his thoughts returned to the letter. He read it two more times, trying to hear what she wasn't saying. That was what his *Urgrossdaddi* Jonah used to say to him before he died— "If you hear what's not being said, you'll hear the heart of the matter."

She'd written, "The minutes began ticking by hours ago, and I continue to wrestle with what to share and what to keep to myself." Clearly, she'd struggled to break through the reluctance he saw when she'd visited. Maybe her inability to talk openly was why she'd asked for them to exchange letters. In person she'd been just another woman, but her letter seemed to have touched something inside him.

While Jonah drove the horse and buggy home after work, Amos cracked jokes. "Two snowmen were standing in a field. One says to the other, 'Funny, I smell carrots too.'"

Cutting and loading lumber for twelve hours straight was exhausting, but Amos rarely seemed tired at the end of a day.

"You don't always have to entertain me."

In a rare moment of seriousness, Amos became still. "But when you laugh, I feel like I've done something to help ease…" He let the sentence drop and stared out the side of the rig.

His brother's past recklessness couldn't be changed. The incident that dogged Amos would never be wiped out, not even through endless moments of amusement. They both knew that. Jonah had forgiven him long before Amos could look him in the eye again, but Amos seemed to find his redemption through the friendship and loyalty he offered Jonah.

"Nothing needs to be eased, Amos."

Amos scratched his face through his whiskers. "When I grow up, I want to be like you."

Jonah chuckled. "You're the oldest of the family, and even your young uns have given up on you growing up."

"Well, aren't you just full of good spirit today? So, you gonna write some of that charm and wit in a letter to that woman?"

Jonah glanced from the road to his brother.

Amos shrugged. "I saw you reading it again at work. Clearly she has your attention."

His brother's statement forced Jonah to think about his emotions. He couldn't deny he had some odd feelings about her. From the moment Pete had placed Beth's business card in his hand and told him of her strong interest in his work, he'd felt a stirring within. And the pleasure of writing to her, sharing parts of himself that he'd not shared with anyone else, and the enjoyment of reading her letter again and again hinted at a possible connection with her. But in person she seemed more like a nervous chicken than an intriguing woman. He supposed that might fade with time.

"Jonah?"

"Maybe."

He pulled into the driveway and let Amos off in front of his home before driving the rig under the overhang. After putting the horse in the pasture, he tossed feed into its trough.

Gazing across the field, he watched a flock of chimney swifts circle above the horizon. At sunset each day they made an odd twittering sound as more birds arrived. Each year, in late summer and early fall, this ritual took place until the flock nearly blackened the sky. Then one evening they wouldn't show up, and he'd know they'd taken off for South America. They were usually gone by now, but perhaps the delay of fall weather had them remaining longer than usual.

Life's mysteries could no more be understood than the thoughts of a flock of birds. The living was ruled by instincts and God-designed principles His creatures had little say over.

And desire.

He reached into his pocket, feeling the letter. Beth wasn't the only one who didn't want to reveal too much. Walking into his shop and to the old part of the building, he thought back to when he'd lost two fingers, full use of one leg, and more than a year of his life.

His siblings suffered nightmares and guilt, but thankfully, that was all. For the lives he'd managed to save, his loss was worth it. Would he have saved any of them had he known the price beforehand? He ran his palm across the dusty leather seat of the sleigh. When he was a teen, his parents had allowed him to decide the sleigh's fate. He'd refused to get rid of it or to use it, so here it sat, making a grown woman think children were hiding under it. It hid things, all right, but childish games and laughter were not part of its secret.

It would take weeks of work to restore the sleigh, and he'd need the help of a blacksmith. He turned to leave. Some things just weren't worth it.

And some were.

He walked the narrow dirt aisle between the stalls of the old building to his workshop bench. He'd created only one other thing since carving the piece Beth bought. A gift box. He'd made it from the same log, but he'd not yet carved it.

He'd tried. Even now, as his hands moved over the rough-hewn treasure, he couldn't visualize what he should carve. That had been the problem for months. Ready to know the thoughts of the man who'd taught him his craft, he tucked the box under his arm.

He went to the barn and hitched a horse to the carriage. As the horse ambled down the road, Jonah leaned back and enjoyed the scenery. Rolling hills, thick foliage on the trees, lush pastures. While looking out over the fields, he let his memory roll back to the day he'd dragged that fallen tree out of the canyon, and he realized just how much he looked forward to writing to Beth.

Pete's driveway came into sight, and he slowed his rig. A few Englischer customers were leaving the store as he got out of the carriage. He noticed they hadn't bought anything. With the box in one hand and his cane in the other, he climbed the steps and went inside.

"Hey, Old Man," Pete called. "How about shutting that door and turning the sign around? I'm done for the day."

It wouldn't matter if Jonah showed up at midnight; Pete never failed to sound pleased to see him. Jonah did as asked and then walked to the counter where Pete stood. In a few minutes they'd walk to the back of the store, go through a doorway, and enter Pete's tiny apartment.

Pete counted money from the cash-register drawer. "What brings you in this time of day?"

Jonah set the box on the countertop.

Pete laid a stack of tens on top of the drawer and moved in front of him. "This looks like it's from that tree you and Amos dragged from the gorge."

"Ya. I've only finished one project from that so far, the one Elizabeth Hertzler bought. Then I made this gift box, but I can't for the life of me carve anything into it."

Pete lifted the box, holding it in his hands as only a fellow carver would—with reverence and respect. He removed the lid and set it on the countertop before running his fingers across the inside of the box. "Maybe you've forgotten the lesson you taught me years ago."

"I taught you?" Jonah knew the old bachelor was getting on in years, but he'd never seen him confused about anything.

"Yep." Pete inspected the box again. "You put a lot of time into this."

"And I'd like to finish it."

Pete reached under the counter and pulled out a soft leather utility case. He unrolled it, revealing a set of carving tools. "You sat right there." He pointed to an old wicker chair near the front counter. "You hadn't been carving more than a year when you made a freestanding bird on a branch—not no relief carving, mind you." Pete walked to his showcase and unlocked it. He brought the bird to Jonah.

"I'd forgotten about making this."

"I won't never forget. Look at the intricate detail. That's not the work of an ordinary kid, or even a man, for that matter. I asked how you made it so lifelike, and you said, 'All I did was remove everything that wasn't the bird.'" Staring at the carving, Pete smiled, making his wrinkles deepen. "You were as wise as an old man from the start."

Jonah passed him the bird. "Whenever I pick up this box to carve on it, I don't see anything."

Pete returned the bird to the showcase and locked it. "Blank?"

Jonah nodded.

"That doesn't sound like you." He pulled a twelve-millimeter gouge with a number four sweep to it from the leather pouch. "You need to remove whatever is hiding the image from you." He placed the tool in Jonah's palm. "The thing is, you may have to cut into more than the box to figure that out."

Jonah squeezed the tool and thought of Beth's letter. The oddness of that piece of wood lying in the forest, tugging at him, and then Beth's strong draw to it felt...eerie. Yet calmness accompanied the feeling, and memories of dragging the felled tree out of the gorge absorbed him.

The cold winter day. The thick layer of snow on the ground. The exhaustion he felt as he wrestled with the elements. Amos calling to him through the frigid air. The strength of the draft horse. The sense of Christmas wonder that filled him once they'd managed to drag the tree out of the canyon.

As he stood in Pete's store, the blank wood in his hands revealed its hidden image. It would take only a few days to create the scene.

But it might be months before he could make himself carve it.

Nine

*B*eth's arms ached from the day's work as she left her parents' home and walked toward the barn. Church would be held there tomorrow, and her Mamm required every bit of help she could get. It wouldn't do for the windows not to be scrubbed clean inside and out, as well as every nook in the house and the old hardwood floors polished to a shine. After doing a thorough cleaning, they'd set up the benches in the living room, so everything was ready for the long Sunday ahead.

The sun was setting, and the early October air had a nip to it as she hitched her horse to the buggy. After climbing into the rig, she slapped the reins and began the four-mile trip back to her place.

With twenty-eight families in their district, nearly three hundred people—including babies, children, and teens—would attend. Thankfully services came to each household in the district only once a year. Unfortunately, Beth had to work just as hard when the rotation landed at her sisters' and brothers' places, as well as Aunt Lizzy's. As a single woman, her life was not her own. It belonged to all her married siblings, her parents, and her aunt.

A wedding for a sibling had been celebrated every other year for the past decade. Refusing the threatening tears, she tried to choke back the sorrow.

Everyone who loved her gently prodded her to lay grief aside. They wanted her to find happiness again, but she never would. Resigned contentment perhaps, eventually. But she couldn't say that to her family.

She longed to tell someone how she really felt and why. But her thoughts and emotions were simply too heavy and too embarrassing to pass on, so she coped the best she could.

She pulled the rig into the barn next to the shop and stepped out of the buggy with wobbly legs. She led the horse to its stall for the night, dumped feed into a trough, and hurried across the yard and into the dry goods store. Too drained to do any office work, she lit a kerosene lamp and slowly climbed the steps.

She had called this stairway "the dark, wooden tunnel" when she was a child. The steps creaked, and the paneled walls seemed to absorb light rather than reflect it.

After setting the lantern on the stand beside her bed, she lit the gas pole lamp, knowing it would give off more than just light. It'd radiate enough heat to knock the chill out of the air. She took hold of the pole and rolled the lamp with her as she entered her tiny kitchen. A package and letter sat on the kitchen table.

Jonah.

Dismal thoughts vanished, like darkness giving way to the power of a match. Snatching up the letter, she noticed it too had been opened. She was ready for her aunt to stop reading her mail from

Jonah. Because of the shared name and business, she and Lizzy often opened each other's mail. Sometimes it didn't matter who opened it; sometimes they didn't know which of them it belonged to. Neither of them ever minded, but Lizzy knew Jonah was writing to Beth, so she had no reason to continue opening the letters.

She unfolded the letter, and the tart flavor of loneliness lost some of its edge.

DEAR BETH,

I THINK I FOUND YOUR LETTER AS FASCINATING AS YOU FOUND MINE. ███████████████████████ ████████████████████████ AND I HOPE WE'RE ABLE TO CONTINUE WRITING FOR A VERY LONG TIME. IF I WERE BOLD AND DARING, I'D CONFESS THAT YOUR LETTER SEEMS TO INDICATE THAT YOU CARRY A HEAVY BURDEN. BUT SINCE I'M NOT BOLD, I WON'T BRING THAT UP.

His joke did little to ease her discomfort. How had he picked up on that? And what had he written that he decided to black out with a marker?

WHAT I DO WANT TO TELL YOU IS THAT WHATEVER YOU SHARE GOES NO FURTHER THAN ME. EVER.

I HAD AN ACCIDENT SOME YEARS AGO AND SPENT A LOT OF TIME IN A HOSPITAL. WHEN I GOT OUT, I BEGAN

*VOLUNTEERING AT OUR AMISH SCHOOL FOR THE DISABLED,
AND I CONTINUE TO THIS DAY TO SPEND TIME WITH THOSE
WHO DEAL WITH PHYSICAL DISABILITIES.*

His life and perspective seemed fascinating. Surely the old man had much in the way of wisdom he could share. Each time she read one line from him, she longed to know five more things.

She opened the cookie jar to see if Lizzy had brought her any goodies today. She had. Homemade chocolate chip. When not cleaning Mamm's house today, Beth had helped prepare both lunch and supper, but she'd not taken the time to eat much of anything.

Munching on a cookie, she began reading again.

*BECAUSE OF MY TIME IN THE HOSPITAL AND REHAB,
I LEARNED THAT JUST AS THERE ARE UNTOLD TYPES OF
INJURIES THAT ALL REQUIRE DIFFERENT TREATMENTS, EACH
PERSON ALSO SUSTAINS INJURIES TO THEIR HIDDEN MAN —
THEIR MIND, WILL, AND EMOTIONS. THEY'RE JUST AS REAL
AS ANY PHYSICAL INJURY, BUT SO OFTEN PEOPLE SEEK HELP
FOR THE BODILY DAMAGE AND IGNORE THE NEEDS OF THE
HEART AND SOUL.*

*THE SPIRIT CAN NO MORE BE IGNORED WHEN IT SUS-
TAINS INJURY THAN A MUTILATED LEG OR SEVERED FINGERS.*

Not only was the man interesting, but he made her feel safe, like it might not be wrong to feel and think and experience life differently than most. Was it possible she could share her oddities with him? Her deepest secrets?

Although her outward life matched most every other Amish woman's existence—from the cape dress and white prayer Kapp to her one-room schoolhouse education—Beth had discovered in the hardest way of all that she didn't possess the tender yet powerful sense of loyalty and love that women should.

Was it possible she could tell Jonah Kinsinger the truth about herself and he'd actually hear her? understand her reality? help her find forgiveness for her sin?

It seemed possible he could be that sort of a man. Older people often had that capability. Sometimes the most accepting, loving people in a person's life were their grandparents, only she was unwilling to unload herself on hers. They'd take it too hard. But a stranger? Surely he could hear her without bearing the weight of her shame. And maybe he'd have wisdom to pass on to her, and she could slip free of the dark blanket that lay heavy over her heart.

Excitement, or maybe hope, seemed to surround her.

You asked how I got that piece of wood out of the canyon. It's quite a tale, and one that tells too much about my stubbornness and not enough about my good sense.

I come from a long line of storytellers (you know the kind: after supper each night they share stories from as far back as the lives of the Amish who escaped

THE PERSECUTION IN THE OLD COUNTRY), SO I WILL WRITE THE EXPERIENCE OUT AS MY OWN URGROSSDADDI MIGHT HAVE DONE IF HE WERE AROUND TO WRITE TO YOU.

SINCE I FAILED TO SHARE ENOUGH OF THE STORY LAST TIME TO SATISFY YOUR CURIOSITY, I WILL OVERDO IT THIS TIME.

STRADDLING MY HORSE, I PEERED DOWN THE SIDE OF THE STEEP RAVINE. I'D BEEN TO THAT SAME SPOT SEVERAL TIMES BEFORE, AND EACH TIME I'D ASSURED MYSELF I COULD FIND A SIMILAR TREASURE IN AN EASIER PLACE TO REACH. BUT THERE I WAS AGAIN.

EVEN THROUGH THE FALLEN SNOW, I SPIED THE TREE.

DISMOUNTING, I FELT EVERY PART OF THE FOREST SUR-ROUND ME—THE EARLY RAYS OF SUNLIGHT WORKING THEIR WAY THROUGH THE CLOUDS OVERHEAD, THE MUSKY SMELL OF ROTTING LEAVES HIDDEN UNDER THE LAYER OF THICK SNOW, AND THE MOVEMENT OF CREATURES I COULDN'T SEE. (MOST OF THE CREEPY-CRAWLIES YOU DON'T LIKE WERE IN HIBERNATION.)

AFTER I REMOVED MY CANE FROM ITS HOLSTER, I TETHERED THE HORSE TO A NEARBY SHRUB AND WALKED TO THE EDGE OF THE DROP-OFF.

BUT HERE I STOOD AGAIN, BRACING MYSELF FOR THE BATTLE OF GETTING MY FIND UP THE SIDE OF THIS CRAG.

HOURS SLIPPED BY LIKE MINUTES, AND I WISHED I'D BROUGHT A STURDIER HORSE, ONE I COULD USE TO HELP

PULL THE CARGO OUT. BUT I HADN'T, AND I COULDN'T RELEASE THE LOAD I'D PULLED HALFWAY UP THE SIDE OF THAT STEEP HILL. MY BODY MOVED AS SLOWLY AS A BOX TURTLE AS I INCHED THE WEIGHT OF MY LOAD UP THE SLIPPERY HILL. I CONTINUED TO MAKE SLOW BUT STEADY PROGRESS AS NIGHT CLOSED IN AROUND ME.

THE CRISP SMELL OF A SNOWSTORM RODE ON THE AIR. BARE TREE LIMBS RUBBED TOGETHER AS THE WIND PICKED UP, AND THE RHYTHM OF THE NIGHT SEEMED TO CHANT.

"GIVE UP."

"GIVE UP."

AS THE SYMPHONY PLAYED, OLD MEMORIES ROSE TO HAUNT ME. THE THING I HATED MOST IN LIFE STOOD BEFORE ME, CLOAKED IN DARKNESS BUT AS REAL AND POWERFUL AS THE LIFE THAT PUMPED THROUGH ME. IT WASN'T THIS SINGLE FIGHT THAT CAUSED THE WORDS OF THE SONG TO HOUND ME. I KNEW THAT. HOW MANY TIMES HAD LIFE SMACKED ME IN THE FACE LIKE I'D RUN INTO THE SIDE OF A BARN? BUT GOD AND I WERE IN AGREEMENT — EVERY VICTORY WAS WORTH FIGHTING FOR.

THE BAD — AND MOST OF THOSE I WORK WITH IN REHAB HAVE HAD PLENTY OF IT — CAN ONLY FIGHT FOR A WHILE. PAIN SUBSIDES. INJURIES HEAL. THEN THE DARKNESS GIVES WAY, LIKE A BULLY FACING SOMEONE TOUGHER. BUT RIGHT THEN, IN SPITE OF MY PEP TALK TO MYSELF, THE CHANTING INSIDE MY MIND HAD ME RATTLED.

"Give up."

"Give up."

I knew that my feelings were lying to me and that I wasn't alone. I shut my eyes, willing the night's clamor to be a sound in my ear and not an echo of the past in my soul. Somewhere above me I heard movement in the forest.

"Jonah!" my brother yelled, sounding hoarse, and I knew Amos had been searching for me for quite a while.

Relief brought new energy, and I angled my head heavenward. "Down here."

Unwilling to chance losing my grip, I kept my heels dug into the terrain. A few moments later Amos yelled my name again. We called back and forth until my brother's voice came from the ridge directly overhead.

"Du feischtielich?"

"Ya. I'm great, but I could use a hand." I tried to see my brother against the dark of night, but I couldn't. "Did you bring the mule?"

"The draft horse."

"Even better. It won't be stubborn."

"Ya, I'll attach this end of the rope to him, and he'll pull you up. You'll have to keep your feet against the face of the crag as much as possible."

Amos tossed one end of a rope over the side of the ravine, but it dangled too far away for me to reach it.

"Uh...I'm not stuck down here. I'm getting what I came for."

The screech of a barn owl came from nearby, and another one responded, but my brother remained quiet for a long minute.

"Fine," Amos finally grumbled. "We won't leave without your precious stump. That's why you came out here alone, wasn't it? You need a better hobby." Amos pulled the rope up and tossed it again, and this time it landed within inches of me. He began mumbling, but his volume assured me he meant every word to be heard. "The best-looking one of the lot, you are. I've been taking your side against the concerns and complaints of the womenfolk for years. And this is how you spend your days? You need a woman!"

"I need what's on the other end of this rope." Although I didn't know why, my gut said it was special. I studied the dangling rope before me and the one in my hand, taut from the stress of the load it held. "Hey, Amos, did you happen to bring two draft horses?"

He hadn't, but we got that tree up the side of

THE STEEP HILL, AND SOON THE HORSE WAS DRAGGING IT OVER SNOWY FIELDS. AND IF LIFE ENDS BEFORE I MAIL THIS LETTER OR LASTS ANOTHER THIRTY YEARS, I'LL ALWAYS BE GRATEFUL THAT PIECE HAS BEEN A BRIDGE FROM YOUR WORK TO MINE.

YOUR FRIEND,
JONAH

Beth's heart thumped like mad, begging for more as she imagined every step of his story. What a beautiful way to share his experience, though the adventure sounded awfully dangerous for a man his age.

She pressed the letter to her chest. He didn't just carve life out of stumps of wood; he carved it into her soul.

Drawing a deep, relaxing breath, she caught a fresh glimpse of the box on the kitchen table. She'd been so interested in reading his letter and so fixed in his words, she'd forgotten about the accompanying gift. Lifting it, she noticed two things: Lizzy hadn't opened it, and Jonah had written a note that read: "From the same tree as the carving you bought." Beth removed the brown paper wrapping and opened the cardboard box.

Inside lay a hand-carved gift box. The image he'd carved thrilled her. She clutched it against herself and hurried down the steps, then ran across the road and let herself in at Lizzy's. The bishop sat across the table from her aunt with a cup of coffee in his hand. Papers were spread on the table between them.

It took only a brief glance to remember her aunt was planning her annual communitywide dinner, dessert, and hayride. Each year she invited all the Amish singles from communities far and wide to come. Those who lived a good distance away would stay for at least one night, often two. For all Lizzy's years of living single, she seemed to have matchmaking in her blood, and many a couple had found each other through these events.

Too excited to ask how the plans were coming, Beth thrust the box toward Lizzy. "Look." She cleared her throat, trying to regain some sense of calm. "Look at what Jonah carved. Did you tell him?"

A look passed between her aunt and the bishop, but Beth didn't care if he minded that Jonah had sent her a carved gift.

Lizzy's eyes brimmed with tears even before she looked at the item. "Tell him what?"

"Is something wrong?" Beth glanced at the bishop.

"The excitement in your eyes and voice." Lizzy rose and cupped Beth's cheeks between her hands. "That's all."

Realizing anew how her sorrow and guilt grieved Lizzy too, Beth hugged her. She'd tried to spare her aunt as much as she could with her silence, but it must not have been enough.

As Beth stepped back, Lizzy wiped the tears from her face. "Let's see what has you glowing." Her aunt peered inside the cardboard box and touched the carved sleigh and its two riders. "No, Beth, I didn't tell him."

Beth brushed her finger along the side of the sleigh. "He even carved sleigh bells just like the etched bronze ones I love so much."

"What didn't your aunt tell him?" Omar asked.

Beth took the box with her as she moved to a kitchen chair. "I know you remember when my family could barely keep food on the table."

"I remember. Blessings galore but hardly any money."

"Well, whenever Daed asked what I wanted for Christmas, I always wanted a sleigh ride. But we didn't own a sleigh, and he must not have known anyone who did, because year after year Christmas came and went without me getting a sleigh ride."

"But he tried other things." Lizzy suppressed a smile.

Recalling half a dozen inventive ideas her father had come up with instead, Beth broke into laughter, and Lizzy joined her. How long had it been since she remembered something fun…and guilt free?

"Ya, he did. One year he fastened a saucer sled behind a horse and put me in his lap." Beth rubbed her head, mocking pain. "If you know anything about saucers, you know we were bound to fly into something at full speed. And we did, but between our heavy clothing and the thick snow, neither of us was seriously hurt."

Lizzy took a mug from the cupboard and filled it with coffee before setting it in front of Beth. "If I remember right, one year he attached a tarp to the back of a wagon, but the rope broke and slung you and your Daed into the road."

"We must have skidded on our backsides twenty feet before stopping." Beth lifted the wooden treasure out of its cardboard box and noticed Jonah had carved scenes all the way around it. When she lifted the lid, she discovered a note.

Dear Beth,

May these scenes fill your mind with serene thoughts so that good dreams follow.

Psalm 4:8 — I will lie down and sleep in peace, for you alone, O Lord, make me dwell in safety.

Jonah

The note made her feel warm and safe, but holding on to any good feelings had been impossible this past year. She'd made her peace with God concerning Henry. That didn't weigh on her. She trusted Him and His judgment. Unfortunately, she didn't trust her emotions or judgment.

Without sharing what Jonah had written, Beth tucked the note back into the gift box. "I should go."

"Don't you want to stay and drink some coffee with us?"

Beth shook her head. "I want to write Jonah. I'll have the buggy hitched at seven thirty in the morning so we can help Mamm get the beds made and the breakfast dishes washed before anyone arrives for church. I'll see you then."

⁂

The air around Lizzy vibrated with hope and fear. When Beth learned the truth about Jonah—which she was bound to do—would she hold a grudge against her like she'd held on to her grief? The question bothered her, but the risk would be worth the price if it helped Beth more than it hurt her.

Lizzy had confessed her deception to Omar, and in spite of his disapproval, he'd not insisted she tell Beth or Jonah. Instead, he'd asked her to pray and to be very careful to hear God.

Omar stirred his coffee, making a clinking sound against the mug. "When will it dawn on her that I'm not visiting this often because of my duties as a bishop?"

Lizzy felt her cheeks turn pink. It seemed too adolescent to be in love for the first time in her long life. "I'm hoping the two of you can work some things out first."

Omar slid his hand toward hers, making her heart pound, but then he stopped and returned it to his lap. His sense of propriety ran deep. He'd not even touched her hand when they were alone, and he couldn't touch her when around others—not yet, maybe not ever. His position as bishop required him to be above reproach, even more than regular folk.

A lopsided smile etched his ruggedly handsome face. "It's not enough that I've spent two years earning your approval. Now I need Beth's too?" There was humor in his voice, but she also heard concern.

"She's the closest thing I'll ever have to a child of my own."

"And she'll always be deeply special to you. She's a part of you and you of her, but we don't know that you'll never have a baby, Lizzy. You're thirty-eight. We've seen women give birth well into their midforties."

"Ya, women who have been having babies half their lives. Their bodies are primed, like a pump that leads to a spring-fed well. And mine is a desert."

A tender, adorable smile radiated from him. "Will you mind too much if we can't have a child of our own?"

Lizzy drew a deep breath, basking in the warmth of the newly burning fire within her. "I never expected to find love. I'll be content forever."

"And after I buried Ruth and spent years raising my children, I never considered I might find love again."

Lizzy's heart turned a flip. Did he practice saying the right thing? "I need you and Beth to...to bond. I don't want to lose a child in order to gain a husband."

"You know that I wish Jonah's work didn't feel like a graven image to me. It's not so much the gift box or wind chimes as those statuelike items he makes. Perhaps I should go see his bishop. Maybe I'd come to see those carvings differently."

"But the bishop is Jonah's own Daed. You could spill my secret without meaning to."

A troubled look removed every hint of a smile, and he went to the coatrack. He took his hat and jacket. "How long will you carry out this secret plan of yours?"

"You saw her tonight. She's on the brink of embracing life again, but she needs more time. I just hope the truth doesn't disclose itself too soon. I had to mark through one of the lines he'd written in his last letter to her. He'd written, 'Your voice on paper sounds so much different than it did in person.'"

"Smart man to figure that out so quickly. And he's in the hands of an amateur romantic." Omar winked at her and put his black hat on. "I'd say this pretense won't last much longer." He moved closer, concern evident in his eyes. "And I pray when it ends, that you are not the one who loses. But whatever happens, I understand what you did and why." He dipped his head once, his eyes glancing to her lips, before returning to her eyes. So many words and feelings ran between them that they were not yet free to express. "Good night, Lizzy."

Ten

*F*eeling hungry, Jonah set his v-tool on the worktable in his living room. His shop was functional, but it was also drafty and physically uncomfortable after a long day at the lumbermill. Rather than sitting on a stool at his workbench, he'd brought the wood into his home.

His desire to carve again had been reawakened by Beth's keen interest in his skill. Once he had the tools in his hands, his passion for the craft seeped back in. After completing her gift box, he'd immediately moved on to another project.

He carried a kerosene lamp to the kitchen, where he lit the eyes to his gas stove, then placed the camp-stove toaster over one and a cast-iron skillet on the other one. He grabbed a loaf of bread and put a slice of bread in two of the four toaster slots before getting a carton of eggs out of the refrigerator.

When someone knocked, he hollered for her to come in. The menfolk walked straight in, so his visitor had to be female—his mother, grandmother, a sister, or a sister-in-law. He cracked an egg into a bowl and glanced up to see his grandmother.

"Hello, Mammi. What brings you out at dinnertime on a drizzly evening like this?"

"You received a letter."

He wiped his hands on a kitchen towel. "Already?"

"Actually it came yesterday, and I planned to pass it to you when you came by, but you never did." She looked around his house. "You're carving again."

"Ya, appears so." He shifted. "The letter?"

"Oh, ya." She pulled her arms free of her black shawl and passed him the envelope.

Just as he expected—as he'd hoped—it was from Beth.

"Jonah." His grandmother's sharp tone made him look up. She hurried to the stove and jammed a fork into a piece of smoking toast. She flung it into the sink and stabbed the other one.

He turned off the stove eye. "Only one side is burnt. The other side is still edible."

She huffed at him and turned on the water. "Not anymore." They laughed, and then she gave him that grandmotherly look of hers. "Why don't you come over to the house? I have plenty of leftovers I can reheat for you. We had beef stew. That'll be better for you and warm your insides."

He wasn't as hungry as he was interested in reading Beth's letter. "I think I'll stay here. If I change my mind, you'll know."

She raised her eyebrows but said nothing else. "All right, then. Good night."

As she left, Jonah opened the letter and removed it from the envelope.

Dear Jonah,

What a great storyteller you are. Since I don't have your gift for words, I can't really share what your letter meant to me. When I opened the package, I couldn't believe my eyes. You see, sleighs have always been a dream and fond memory of mine. I'm so excited to have another item made from the wood you dragged out of that canyon. Although I must confess you do sound, as you said yourself, extremely stubborn.

The beauty of that box and of your friendship means so much.

We were very poor during most of my childhood. I had one Christmas wish year after year—to ride in a sleigh. But in spite of his best and sometimes dangerous efforts, my Daed could not make that Christmas dream come true. By the time I turned eight, I understood the constraints of money and made a point to always ask for something my father could provide. So I'd choose something from my aunt's store, like a few yards of fabric for a new dress or a favorite piece of candy. That way he could buy it at cost.

One Christmas Eve after my married siblings had gone home and my younger ones had gone to bed, my father went to my uncle's home to gather the gifts for Christmas morn...or so I thought. At the request of my mother, I stood on the porch, cleaning snow and ice off the steps so my father wouldn't fall when he returned.

I was eighteen years old, but when I heard sleigh bells,

I felt like a hopeful child again. I remember standing in place, absorbing the joy of it. Isn't it funny how certain things mean so much to us for so little reason? What would make a child want a sleigh ride so badly? Or a nearly grown woman feel such joy at the sound of distant sleigh bells?

As the jingle grew closer, I thought my feet might come off the ground. I truly did. All I wanted was to see the sleigh pass, but when it came into view, it slowed and pulled into our driveway. I wish you could have seen my father's face as he finally brought me the one thing I'd always wanted for Christmas.

My mother brought a thermos of hot chocolate out to us and an armload of blankets. The sleigh was not due back to the owner until midmorning, and we rode nearly all night, singing carols and talking of the God who provides. We were able to take my younger siblings for a ride after they opened their presents. But the greatest gift was knowing that my Daed loved me enough to care about a silly girl's child-hood Christmas wish.

Under the weight of the last few years, I had forgotten things you have caused me to remember. I'm not sure how, but sadness and guilt have a way of changing a person. You've judged me correctly, though I can scarcely see how when we know so little of each other. I do carry a secret. A horrid one.

I think you must be right, that just as there are physical

injuries that cause permanent injury, so it is with damage to the inner man.

My problem began the day I realized I could not do what I'd promised to do. I wrestled with myself for a while, and then I went to Henry and told him my decision. I was willing to pay the price, but he paid instead, and I shall never be free of that guilt—no more than he can be free of the grave.

I'm healthy in body but still heartbroken in so very many ways. I try to hide that from those who love me—not because I fear their judgment. I have allowed God to judge me already, but I don't want to hurt them.

I began this letter in great joy, but I end it sobbing like a child. It seems you have the power to stir my heart and my memory with your carving. And loosen my pen with the sincerity of your letter.

If I dare mail this letter, I will be surprised. But I have written my secret. Perhaps vaguely, but it is done.

Beth

Jonah eased into a chair. Although he was unsure exactly what she was talking about, her words held the weight of a dozen silos.

"Beth." As he whispered her name, he couldn't visualize the woman who'd sat across from him in the gazebo. The two voices, the Beth from the gazebo and the Beth who wrote to him, were very different. No doubt.

He closed his eyes, seeing nothing but blank darkness. He tried to relax and wait on an image to form, like he did when carving, but nothing came to him. Recollections from the time Beth had visited and the things she'd later written to him swirled like drops of oil in water, but no matter how he looked at it, they wouldn't blend into one person.

The woman in his gazebo said she knew someone who was struggling. It'd be easy to believe this letter was from that person, but would Elizabeth Hertzler have deceived him?

Pulling the card Pete had given him out of his wallet, he thought about calling her. But then guilt covered him. She'd just laid bare her heart, shared the hardest thing of her life to him, and he doubted her?

He glanced at the letter. No, he didn't doubt the woman who'd written to him. He heard her sincerity as she unveiled her soul. He read the letter again and stumbled over the words "my aunt's store."

Her aunt's store?

It was possible the store she now ran had once belonged to her aunt, but…something left him ill at ease. A call would set things right. He looked at the clock. Just past six. He didn't know what her store hours were, but if it wasn't closed already, it would be soon. It'd take him a good twenty minutes to get to Pete's to use his phone.

Willing to take the chance, he slid into his jacket and hat and headed for the barn. The rain came and went in spurts, but his horse made good time. When he arrived at Pete's, the store was closed. He knocked and a minute later saw Pete coming out of his office. Pete unlocked the door.

"Hey, Old Man. What happened to your key?"

"I didn't think to bring it. I need to use your phone."

"Sure. You know where it is. Care to eat a bite of supper with me when you're done?"

"Who's cooking? Me or you?"

"You. Oh, did I mention that I'm glad you stopped by?"

Jonah chuckled and moved to the phone behind the cash register. He dialed the number and waited.

"Hertzlers' Dry Goods."

Nothing in the woman's voice sounded familiar. "Yes, I'm trying to reach Beth Hertzler."

"You've reached her. How can I help you?"

She sounded young and friendly, and he felt rather queasy. "I don't think you're the right person. I spoke to the woman I'm trying to reach and…"

"Oh, well, two Elizabeth Hertzlers run this store. I'm one of them, and my aunt is the other. You must've spoken to Lizzy, but I'm Beth."

His mind ran with thoughts, but he urged it to pick up the pace. As dozens of pieces of his encounter with Elizabeth Hertzler shuffled around inside him, he remembered her saying, "You should write to Beth. I mean…Beth, Lizzy, Elizabeth—they're all forms of my name."

Suddenly feeling like an idiot, Jonah tried to find his voice. "Lizzy?"

"Yes, that's my aunt. The store is closed for the night, so she's not here, but if it's store business you need her for, I'd be glad to try to help you."

A sense of betrayal burned through him, but until he got to the bottom of this, he'd not say a word to anyone but Lizzy about it. "Uh, no, I shouldn't bother you."

"It's no bother. I wouldn't have answered if I wasn't at my desk. Is there an order you'd like to check on or place?"

Tempted to voice the questions that pounded at him, he resisted. Who did she think she was writing to? "No, but thanks."

"Can I get your name and number so I can pass the info to Lizzy?"

"No, I'm good. I don't think I need anything from her after all."

The woman grew quiet, probably taken aback by the oddness of this conversation.

"Good-bye, Beth."

"Bye."

Jonah hung up the phone, feeling like he knew far less now than when he'd arrived.

"Whoa." Pete scratched his head. "For a man who's slow to anger, you sure do look riled."

"You talked to Elizabeth Hertzler face to face, right?"

"Sure did. She's a bit odd for an Amish woman."

"Odd how?"

"All businesslike, maybe? I don't know." He shrugged. "It's hard to explain the difference, but I've had Amish women come in here my whole life. They tend to be quiet when dealing with men. They ask careful questions, barely hinting at the tougher ones inside them concerning some piece I have that they're interested in, and when I answer, they always seem to keep their real thoughts to themselves. The one you're talking about had a polite salesman-type boldness about her. And she didn't mind questioning my methods as the owner of the store, especially when it came to your carving."

"What did she look like?"

"Well, it's been a while, but…I remember she had dark hair. And even though it was August when she was here, her skin was as fair as if it were the middle of winter, so I didn't reckon she spent much time in a garden."

"Her age, Pete. How old was she?"

"Oh, well, why didn't you say so?" He scratched his head again, looking like his memory was being taxed. "Young. A couple years younger than you, maybe more."

Wavering between anger and confusion, Jonah felt his head pounding. "You're sure? I mean, she didn't look a few years older rather than younger?"

"There was no way she was older than you."

As the woman's trickery continued to dawn on him, his face flushed with embarrassment. "Anything else?"

"Not that I remember. What's going on?"

"Not sure, but I can guarantee I don't like it."

"Are you going to try to figure it out?"

"I'll need to think awhile before I know the answer to that."

Eleven

*L*izzy closed the door to the office and phoned Pete's. She knew the minute Beth told her about the strange conversation she'd had with a man who had their names mixed up that Jonah had figured out what was going on. What had once seemed like an opportunity to help Beth now loomed over her as the utter deceit that it was. She'd tried to reach him on three separate days but hadn't been successful. During the last call Pete gave her a set time, saying he'd try to have Jonah at the store then.

As the phone rang over and over again, her nervousness made her feel lightheaded. It'd already stolen her sleep over the past few days. She couldn't blame Jonah for not wanting to talk to her, but if she didn't connect with him today, she'd get Gloria to take her to his place. If she could've gotten away from the store over the last few days, she would have. But regardless if she talked to him today or tomorrow, how would she explain her actions?

Finding it hard to stay on the line, she shivered when someone picked up the receiver.

"Pete's Antiques."

She recognized Pete's voice easily by this point. "This is Lizzy Hertzler. Is Jonah there?"

"He is. Don't want to be, but I cornered him into it. Hang on, and I'll go get him."

Unable to pray, she hoped to find a way to tap into the man's understanding and forgiveness. While rapping her fingers on the desk, she noticed one of the invitations to the fall hayride.

"This is Jonah."

The distance in his voice said even more than his unfriendly greeting.

"Uh, this is Elizabeth Hertzler. Lizzy."

He said nothing. If she could just speak with him face to face, she could find the right words to make him understand. She hated the phone. It just wasn't the right way to communicate heartfelt emotions.

"I know you're angry, and you have a right to be, but I really need us to sit down together and talk. I'm sure you're wondering why I did what I did. And I'll explain everything but not on the phone. I have a fall hayride each year. Single young people from all over come for that. Why don't you—"

"No, I'm good. Thanks."

Lizzy's heart sank. She couldn't blame Jonah. She fought against tears and managed to find her voice again. "I know I wasn't honest, and you're right to be angry." She grabbed a tissue off Beth's desk and tried to hide the sounds of her crying from him.

"However funny you've found this game of yours, it's not."

"Please don't think anyone's been laughing at you. My reasons are complicated, and I—"

"So," Jonah interrupted, "who all knows about this hoax?"

"Me and Omar. He's a close friend and our bishop, and he's had deep concerns about my actions from the start. But for too long I've looked in Beth's eyes and seen nothing but pain, like staring at a wounded doe. I've been desperate to find some way to help her. Then she came home from her buying trip this summer with your carving. Excitement radiated from her eyes and voice for the first time in more than a year, and all she wanted was to get permission to carry your work in our shop or be allowed to market it to Englischer shops."

"And just who does she think she's writing?"

"You. Only a very old you."

"So you led her to believe she's writing to my grandfather."

"Well, no, not exactly. Pete called you Old Man, and that's who she thinks you are. I told her the truth—that you've never married and you live by yourself. She thinks you're a lonely old man. Your work reaches into her and stirs life. You can't imagine what that spark of excitement in her did to me. I didn't set out to trick anyone, but when I met you, I knew you could help."

"I still don't understand why you didn't simply tell both of us the truth about the other one."

"If I'd told you my plan, would you have agreed to write to Beth without revealing who you were?"

"Absolutely not."

"And if she'd known you were a young, single man, I would have met resistance with the strength of ten oxen. She wouldn't have read your letters or written to you."

"Why?"

The office door opened, and Beth walked in. Lizzy covered the receiver. She had hoped for some privacy while Beth was too busy with customers to take any real notice.

Lizzy lowered the phone from her ear. "I'll just be another minute."

"No problem. Mr. Jenkins is here, and I need his invoice." She pointed to the phone and went to the file cabinet. "No need to keep the person waiting."

Unwilling to reveal her secret to Beth or to let go of this chance, Lizzy held the phone to her ear. "Please come to the hayride event. It's this Saturday night. We're having a dinner at five and an evening of hayrides, bonfires, and fun. People start showing up right after lunchtime. A lot of the young people will stay with me until Sunday afternoon, some until Monday. You're more than welcome to stay however long you wish."

Beth moved in front of the desk. "Be honest, Lizzy. Tell that poor soul there'll be plenty of food and very little rest and that, although their goal may be fun, your goal is matchmaking." Her niece raised an eyebrow, seeming to dare Lizzy to dispute what she'd said.

"Mind your manners," Lizzy whispered.

She shrugged and set the file of invoices on the desk, looking through the stack of papers.

"If you're uncomfortable," Lizzy continued, hoping to keep her cover, "you'll blend in with dozens of other people. There are always new people we've never met before. It's the best way to get this sorted out."

Beth rolled her eyes. "And the matchmaking begins."

Lizzy had no doubt that even Jonah heard the disdain in her niece's voice. She lowered the phone. "Could you take your wet-blanket attitude elsewhere for just a minute please?"

"I was just warning the poor girl." She winked at Lizzy before she left, closing the door behind her.

"So now I'm a girl?" Jonah sounded as if he found Beth's description amusing, and Lizzy hoped she was making headway. Still, his voice reflected leeriness and anger.

"Jonah, please don't do anything that will hurt Beth. I know she has to be told, but she's had a spark to her of late, and she's innocent in this. Just come to the event and we'll talk. I doubt if she'll participate. You have wisdom, and I wanted her to hear it, but she wouldn't have if she'd known you were a single guy not much older than she is. Will you come this weekend and give us a chance to talk?"

"Maybe. I need to think about it."

<hr />

Pete's nephew, Derek, stopped his car outside Hertzlers' Dry Goods. Jonah studied the store, still not sure he should have come. The hitching post had five horses tied to it, and the parking lot held eight parked cars.

"Busy place." Derek put the gearshift in neutral. "Uncle Pete might not see this much traffic in a month sometimes."

Jonah nodded and looked across the street. Long lines of horseless buggies were parked in the field. Two volleyball nets were set up, and young people were laughing while playing the game.

Feeling old and out of place, he flipped the lock. "It looks like the get-together is happening across the road. I'll be waiting for you in front of that house in two hours."

"Uh, yeah, I should be back by then."

Jonah didn't like Derek's sudden uncertainty on their agreed timing, but there was little he could do now. If Pete still had a license, Jonah would have asked him to drive here today. But Pete had eyesight issues that had made him give up driving.

With his cane in hand, Jonah got out of the car and headed across the street to the house. The yards—side, front, and back—teemed with young singles. A couple of older men stood at an industrial-sized grill, smoke billowing from it as they cooked what smelled like chicken. A baseball game was under way in the pasture, a portable dog cage acting as a backstop. The late-October air had a nip to it, and everyone had on sweaters or light jackets.

Before he was halfway across the paved road, Lizzy came out the front door of the house. With a platter in her hands, she went down the porch steps and into the side yard. She passed the platter to a man standing at the grill.

On her way back to the porch, she spotted Jonah heading her way. "You came." Her smile held uncertainty.

"I came. It's a bit busy around here."

"Ya." She stood in front of him, studying his face. "I hope you can come to understand why I did such a deceitful thing."

He remembered the first time he'd met Lizzy. The earnestness in her eyes and voice were obvious. But did she fully realize Beth could end up more wounded rather than less?

When he said nothing, she motioned for them to walk to a set of chairs. A game of volleyball was being played twenty feet away on one side of them, and at about the same distance on their other side was a game of horseshoes. Dozens of young people stood watching, talking, and cheering.

Jonah placed his elbows on the armrests. "Tell me what you'd hoped to accomplish by having me and Beth write to each other."

"When we met, you seemed to understand how to deal with loss and pain. She suffered loss, and because of that, she has walled everyone out. I thought your letters might share some much-needed balance and that by keeping your identity a secret, she stood a chance of hearing what someone has to say."

"And that would make what you've done worth it?"

"I hoped so." Lizzy leaned in. "But I can recognize that it was a careless idea—wrong and hurtful. Even if it's what I thought Beth needed. Can you forgive me?"

"I have forgiven you, Lizzy, but—"

Her hand covered his. *"Gross Dank, un Gott segen dich."* Her eyes brimmed with tears as she gave thanks and said, "God bless you."

"Gern Gschehne. Unfortunately, forgiving you solves nothing."

"I know Beth will be upset with me, and I can't imagine what she'll say or do. But she connected with you through your work, and you two shared letters. How angry can she be?"

"She thinks she's been writing to a grandfather. Imagine her embarrassment and anger when she discovers you lied to her."

Lizzy's mouth moved a few times before she managed to speak. "Did she confide things in you?"

Jonah wasn't about to answer that. "She had a right to choose who she would turn to, Lizzy. And I shouldn't have been pulled into this, thinking it was one kind of a relationship. You offered friendship, remember? Then you made me someone's counselor."

Lizzy stared into the sky and wiped at several stray tears. "You're right."

A flock of young people passed nearby, every bit as flighty and noisy as chimney swifts.

"Is she here?"

Lizzy shook her head. "She's working."

The constant buzz and laughter made him wonder what secret was so strong it could keep Beth from embracing life again. "I'd like to get out of this without embarrassing or hurting her."

A clamor of excited voices caught his attention. A group of five or six girls headed toward them. One glimpse at the girl at the back of the group, and Jonah stopped breathing.

The woman from Pete's store. The one who'd nearly run into him. The one he hadn't been able to forget.

As everything he knew fell into place, emotions tugged at him—shock, frustration, amazement, embarrassment, and even honor that she valued his work so highly.

Her deep blue eyes were the most amazing he'd ever seen, not because of their beauty, but because of the unknown riches he believed lay behind them.

"Look who I dragged out of her office," one of the girls yelled as she tugged on the arm of *the* girl, of Beth.

The games and conversations paused, and people broke into a disorganized murmur of welcomes, claps, and cheers.

"Denki." Beth lifted her chin and made three circular motions with her hands as she bowed. An uproar of cheers rose into the air. "Denki. Ya, if someone drags me, I'll show up." She gave one slow nod. "Now, please shut up and go back to talking and playing."

Her friends laughed, but most did as they were told. The girls surrounding her slowly dispersed, and the sight of black fabric engulfed him.

She stopped at one of the grills on the far side of the yard and spoke to a man. Then she spotted Lizzy and headed toward her.

What would he say to her? How would he and Lizzy tell her?

Beth stopped before them, lifting a hand to shade her eyes from the sun. "Lizzy, Daed said to tell you the meat is almost done."

What Jonah saw in Lizzy's eyes during those few moments explained a lot about her. She loved Beth dearly, enough to take a chance at angering both Beth and him. Lizzy stood. "Honey, I'm surprised you came today."

Beth shrugged. "Susie and Fannie said Daed asked me to come, and then they proceeded to drag me."

Lizzy put her arm around Beth's shoulders. "There's someone here you should meet."

Beth looked right at him, and he saw a hint of recognition flash through her eyes, as if she might be trying to place him. "Hello." The friendliness he'd seen in her when addressing the group was gone; instead she sounded like the businesswoman Pete had told him about.

"Beth." Lizzy's voice shook. "I'd like you to meet—"

Noise exploded among the volleyball players. Beth's brows furrowed, but she held out her hand. Her palm was soft against his rough calluses. He'd thought about this woman every day since seeing her at Pete's. If he'd stood any chance of making friends with her, Lizzy had ruined it.

"Hi, Beth."

Judging by the look in her eyes when she shook his hand, she hadn't heard his name, leaving him torn about repeating it or letting the matter drop for now. It seemed a very inappropriate time to share such awkward and upsetting news. Lizzy didn't seem to know what to do either.

The volume around them rose again.

"Lizzy, I'm going back to the store now," Beth said. "Okay?"

"Already?"

"I did as Daed asked." A captivating half smile graced her lips, and she raised one eyebrow. "Besides…" She slid the letter he'd written from the bib of her apron. After talking to Lizzy on the phone, he'd had to write Beth again. If he hadn't, she might think her openness had caused him to stop writing.

Lizzy looked at Jonah. His insides churned like the stew children made when playing—a concoction of muddy water swirling with dirt and debris, only good for pretending. He didn't want to play make-believe. Never had but especially not now.

With Lizzy watching him, Beth's attention moved to him too. But rather than showing interest in who he was and why he seemed familiar, her features grew cooler.

She kissed her aunt's cheek. "I'll see you tomorrow afternoon, okay?"

"Maybe." Lizzy winked at her.

Beth's lips pursed. "Don't send Daed or my sisters to come get me after supper. I'm not going to the bonfire. Is that clear?"

Lizzy shrugged. "This kind of gathering where I invite Amish from all over happens only once a year, Beth."

"Good night, Lizzy."

He watched her as she headed for the road. "We would have eventually met on our own, you know."

"How?"

"I didn't know her name, but I ran into her at Pete's. He now orders things from her for his store. We would have met properly soon enough. By then she'd be past such grief, and we wouldn't have all the difficulties you've put in our path."

"You don't understand. *I* don't understand. Something changed her, and…" Lizzy shook her head. "I shouldn't have said that much.

But it wouldn't have worked—not since Henry. She's become a brick wall. She's unyielding when it comes to those who might be interested in her. Are you?"

"Am I what?"

"Interested."

"I wouldn't know. Would you expect me to be?"

"You seem a bit intrigued."

"She's beautiful. But a lot of women are." Even as he answered Lizzy, he knew he felt a definite awareness of Beth—had since the day he saw her at Pete's. And now to realize she was the one his work called to, the one writing him letters. His sense of awe grew.

Confused, he watched as Beth continued to make her way toward the road. She walked backward as a group of girls spoke with her. Each time she broke free of one conversation, someone else called and ran closer to talk to her. He couldn't help but chuckle. Just as she made it to the road, the man she'd spoken to at the grill, the one she referred to as her Daed, called to her.

Beth turned. As they talked, her eyes moved to Jonah and settled there. After several long moments she looked at the man in front of her, responded to something he'd said, hugged him, and then crossed the road. But she didn't go inside the store. She walked down a path, opening the letter as she went.

The beauty of the image—huge beech trees holding a golden canopy above her while she read his letter—only added to his confusion. His last letter wasn't warm or filled with stories, and he regretted that. He'd been trying to be fair to Beth while getting free of the mess Lizzy had pulled him into, but now he wished he'd been less distant.

Lizzy cleared her throat. "I'm so sorry for what I've done, Jonah. I only thought of Beth, and even then I aimed for the insights you had to offer that might help her. I didn't really think about all the possible emotional ties."

"I know, Lizzy. Stop apologizing."

"She didn't catch your name, did she?"

"Appears not."

"When I met you, I was willing to do anything to help her. And now I fear I've done the opposite."

"And for good reason."

Twelve

*L*izzy opened her stove and pulled out a pan of rolls. In spite of her many guests, she'd never felt so alone. She'd held on to her optimism that when Beth learned the truth, it might work out smoothly somehow, but now that she'd witnessed her niece's reaction to Jonah, she knew it had been a false hope. Beth had shown no measure of openness toward him, and Jonah might find it easier to break through a solid oak door with his bare hands than to remain—or was it to become?—friends.

Lizzy could blame no one but herself, but she wanted a bit of comfort, which meant finding Omar. It was ridiculous to feel this way. She'd been a single adult, running her own life, for nearly twenty years. Whether her decisions were wise or stupid, she'd borne the weight of them without the arms of a man to shore her up. So why was this ache to be with him so strong that she couldn't ignore it?

Tears threatened, and she grabbed her thickest sweater and slipped out the back door. At the second eight-foot grill, Omar stood without his coat on, basting chicken in barbecue sauce. It seemed a little cool not to have on a jacket. She moved in his direction, and the crowd of young people filling her yard seemed to fade away.

As if a match had been struck at midnight, she understood a dozen things about herself. She wasn't worthy to become the wife of a bishop. She'd been meddlesome and used trickery to cover her deceit.

When Omar's eyes met hers, her composure broke. Tears ran down her cheeks.

He moved to her. *"Was iss letz?"*

The concern in his eyes as he asked what was wrong magnified her emotions. She shouldn't be here, not if they meant to keep their relationship quiet. They'd agreed not to tell anyone until the time was right. Although they weren't sure when that would be, they knew they'd know when it arrived—like knowing a hayfield was ready or the corn was ripe. Now she wondered if that time would ever come, because it seemed that Omar should be free of someone as foolish as she was.

He turned to Stephen. "Can you watch this grill? I'll be back in just a few minutes."

"Ya."

He placed his hand under her forearm and guided her toward the carriage barn. "Kumm." He opened the wooden door, and they stepped inside.

She paced back and forth in front of him. "I saw it, Omar. I saw the reason I meddled in Beth's life. Why I lied to Jonah about who he was writing to. Even why I do these get-togethers year after year. And it scares me."

"What did you see?"

"I thought it was because of what Beth needed. But that's not it."

Her ego lunged forward, urging her not to say more, but she would. "I don't want *anyone* spending their life alone, not if they don't have to. All this time I thought I'd accepted God's providence in the way my life went. I even thought I liked it. But now I discover…"

Omar stood in front of her, blocking her pacing. "That you've been lonelier than you knew?"

She nodded. "Beth was the best thing to ever happen to me. She filled my days like a daughter, and I wanted to prevent her from making wrong decisions."

"All parents have to learn that a child's path must be his or hers to choose, not Mamm's or Daed's to manipulate."

"But what if my life has influenced hers too much? She attached herself to me before she was school age, and even before Henry I was afraid she'd want to follow my lead and live as a single businesswoman."

Omar stepped closer. "I don't think Beth's struggles are because of who you are. I think she's strong enough to get past what's ailing her, with or without your"—he mockingly cleared his throat—"help."

The longer she stood there, the more she knew that Omar deserved someone better. "What am I going to do if Beth gets hurt and it's my fault? Or if she's so angry she won't even talk to me?"

He placed his hands on her shoulders. "Beth's a hard one to figure out, but she loves you."

She lowered her head. "That's not the only reason I'm upset."

He placed his warm fingers under her chin and tilted her face upward. "What else weighs on you?"

Fresh tears broke free. "I'm not worthy to be the wife of a bishop."

"And I'm not worthy to be a bishop, but judging by how God

replied to Moses when he said something similar, I don't think He wants us wasting time moaning about it."

"You need someone better, Omar."

"And there will be times after we're married when you'll think the same thing—that you need someone better than me. I assure you of that."

"Are you hearing me?"

"I am. You're burdened with guilt over your dishonesty with Beth and Jonah. And because of that, you're tempted to ruin all my future happiness."

He placed his hands in hers, making her distress melt into a pool of warm security.

"I love you, Lizzy Hertzler. And I'm glad you're not perfect, because when we marry, it'd be awful to be the only one who's ever wrong. I'll tell you the truth. You wouldn't have wanted to be my first wife, because I thought I was always right about everything. It took a long time for me to see that a head of a household or a head of several church districts can be just as wrong as anyone else."

Desire swept through her at his openness, and she stood on her tiptoes and kissed his cheek. "You're something else nowadays. Ya?"

"I'm something all right."

She chuckled. "I'd better go."

<hr />

Jonah had little to say as he sat at the supper table, but he enjoyed the banter. Tables filled every room in the house. The food and laughter during the meal held a pleasure of their own. He lost track of the conversation a few times due to differences in the region's Pennsylvania Dutch. Each state, and sometimes each area, had its own dialect of the language. When not trying to decipher the unfamiliar words, he met a lot of people, including Beth's Daed, a married brother who'd been helping grill meat, and two of her sisters, still young enough to be in their *rumschpringe*—their running-around years.

"I'm not going to the bonfire without Bethie," Fannie, the older of the two sisters, boldly stated to those at the table. "Not again this year."

It wasn't long before ten or twelve of those near her agreed. They'd take a wagon across the road and refuse to leave until she joined them. Jonah wanted to see who would win this battle.

After dinner he stepped out onto the front porch. Sunlight had faded, and a golden harvest moon hung on the horizon. Through a second-story window of the store, he saw the dim glow of a kerosene lamp.

When everyone had boarded a chosen hay-filled wagon, he watched as one wagonload of youth went across the road and parked in the grass under the window where the light shone. They taunted Beth by calling her name over and over again. A minute later she came onto the porch, leaned over the railing so she could peer around the side of the house, said her piece, and went back inside. He might have laughed, but the need to tell her the truth blocked all possibility of levity.

Lizzy joined him on the porch. "What are they doing?" She pointed at two young men who'd gotten out of the wagon. One had a baseball bat, and the other pitched a ball to him, using the side of the store as a backstop.

Lizzy pulled her sweater tighter around her. "Those teens have gotten caught up in their fun-time mood and aren't thinking. Come with me."

He followed her down the stairs and across the street.

"*Schtobbe!*" Her command to stop was interrupted by the sound of breaking glass and a yelp from inside the building. The guys ran around the side of the house, heading for the porch of the store, but Lizzy beat them to it.

"No way. You keep that bat and your wildness out of the store. Gross Dank." She looked through the small crowd until her eyes found Jonah. "Jonah, check on Beth and the damage, please."

He wasn't sure of his motive, but he wasted no time going inside. A second-story window had been broken by the foul ball, so he looked for a set of steps. A glance through one door revealed a small office. His carving took up a third of her desk. He opened another door and found the stairs. With the aid of his cane, he soon stood at the open door of a small apartment, tapping on it.

Beth called out to him from another room. "I don't think the idea of a home run is to hit the ball into someone's home and then run."

She didn't sound angry, but he couldn't really tell.

"Jake Glick, if you want this ball, you'll come in here and help clean up this mess." Her tone sounded like a big sister correcting a sibling.

Jonah eased inside, feeling odd standing in her bedroom, but it was just inside the threshold of the stairway. Her voice came from his right, a kitchen by the looks of it. He moved to the doorway.

"You know, there are better ways of getting my little sister's atten—" Beth looked up and stopped midsentence. "You're not my sister's beau."

"I realize that." He hoped she took his words as he meant them, like a playful tease.

Suppressing a smile, she placed several large pieces of glass into a trash can.

He gripped his cane, easing some pressure off his bad leg. "Lizzy wouldn't let the culprits come into her store."

Beth grabbed the ball from the table and tossed it to him. "For their sake or the store's?"

He caught it, feeling the sting of the force from her throw. "Well, I thought for the store's, but I'm beginning to wonder…"

She blinked, and then a sweet, genuine smile shone through, hinting at the woman he thought her to be. "They'll want that ball back, and now you have it."

Amused at her polite dismissal, he tossed the ball through the broken window. "And now they have—"

"Ouch," someone bellowed from below.

Beth's beautiful eyes grew large, and she covered her mouth with her hand as she moved to the window.

"Denki," a young man's voice said cheerfully.

Beth waved at someone below, and when she looked back at

Jonah—her eyes filled with mischievous humor—they both broke into laughter.

A stack of paper lay on the table beside the lantern. His name was written across the top of one page, but it had no other words. The gift box he'd carved sat beside her pen. He dreaded the thought of telling her who he was, but he had no choice.

Procrastinating, he misdirected the conversation. "You don't do hayrides, Beth?"

She shrugged. "Not anymore."

"You think you've outgrown them?"

"Mostly I fear for those who will think they've found the right person to build a life with before the night is through."

"And you're sure they'll be wrong?"

She shrugged again.

He grabbed a broom from the corner. "I know you have an opinion."

"How can you possibly *know* that?" She placed the dustpan on the floor.

With gentle caution he swept shards into it. "Because your eyes said so."

Her head tilted downward so that she wasn't looking at him, but her aura, as deep and rich as her letters, filled the air. "I can tell you, but you won't like me at all once I do."

Unable to imagine not liking this woman, he chuckled. "I'd like to know."

"The men go because they hope to find a girl who will always be like she is now. They hope her beauty will never change and her attention will stay fully centered on him the way it is tonight. And the girls go in hope of finding a man who will always be as gentlemanly and kind as he is on the hayride." She took a pan full of glass to the trash and dumped it. "True love has more facets than a lifetime can explore. I've seen it. But it's not found in nights like tonight—where strangers meet and sparks fly."

He wondered why she felt so sure of her opinion. "But if it's impossible for love to start through the meeting of two people, where is it found?"

When she raised an eyebrow, seemingly growing leery of him, he knew it was time to stop the small talk and tell her the truth. There wouldn't be a better time.

"I need to—"

"Beth. Beth. Beth." The chant started again, rattling the remaining broken glass in the window's frame.

She growled softly. "I thought they'd left for the bonfire by now." She motioned toward the door. "Go, and tell them I'm not coming."

"The window needs boarding up. It's going to be a very cool night."

"I'll handle it. Just go convince them that they can't annoy me into going."

"But we need to talk."

When a look of concern flashed through her eyes, he knew he'd stepped too close, but she tried to cover her discomfort with a polite smile. "We've talked plenty, but denki."

The wind carried the chant through the window. "Beth. Beth. Beth."

"Please." She elongated the word.

Part of him wanted to leave, to not tell her anything. Not yet. It made sense to wait until Lizzy wasn't so busy with guests and, if Beth had a screaming fit, until there weren't so many to hear her private business.

"Beth," a man called from the foot of the steps.

"Ya, Daed?" she hollered.

"I heard you have a busted window." His heavy footsteps started up the stairway.

She turned to Jonah. "See, I have help with the window. What I need is that crowd to leave me alone."

As he paused, watching her, his moments with her seemed suspended inside him like specks of gold dust—from the encounter at Pete's, to the letters they'd shared, to each second he'd been with or seen her today. He felt more drawn to her than he'd ever imagined possible.

He forced himself to leave, deciding that the best way to reveal the truth was by letter. He'd find Lizzy and tell her to let him break the news to Beth.

Thirteen

*B*eth moved to the window and watched as the man who'd been in her room stood in the yard, speaking to the group in the wagon, hopefully persuading them to go on without her.

Most of them looked up at her and waved. She smiled and returned the friendly gesture. The buggy pulled onto the main road and slowly gained speed. The nameless man spoke with Lizzy for a moment before she climbed into a wagon and left with the young people. He then walked toward Lizzy's house, and Beth couldn't make herself pull away from the window.

Her thoughts blended into each other. Lizzy's casting net for bringing Amish singles from far and wide drew first-timers to this event year after year, but Beth still couldn't believe he'd come. She had no recollection of his cane, but she remembered the man. His brown eyes, the colliding emotions inside her, the way he'd stood inside Pete's store, studying her as she had studied him. She'd embarrassed herself with how attracted she was to him. At least this time she'd kept her wits.

Through broken glass she kept her vigil. The cane and his slower amble only added to the sense of charm and intrigue he carried. Despite her past and her will, something about him drew her. But she'd felt a spark for Henry too—not nearly as strong, but it had been there.

Mourning Henry had so little to do with missing him and so much to do with guilt. When he was found dead, the police had asked her questions, and she'd answered honestly. But they didn't ask the right ones. The coroner declared his death an accident, and in a court of law it was. But no judge or jury had asked her to testify to her part in his fatal injury.

An odd sadness enveloped her, as if the reality of who she'd become was sinking in afresh. Fear and blame owned her now, and there was no way to buy herself free.

The man moved to the porch and sat, placing his cane beside him and his forearms on his knees. When he looked up at her, it felt like a part of her flew through the window and met a part of him, dancing on the wind for a brief moment.

Refusing to keep staring at him, she turned from the window. She grabbed a wet cloth and wiped a few stray shards of glass from her kitchen table, but thoughts of the man pulled on her.

She eased to the window again, hoping he wouldn't see her. A car pulled into Lizzy's driveway, and he walked toward it.

Her father stepped up behind her. "If he's that interesting, perhaps you should go talk to him."

The man looked up at her again.

Move away from the window, Beth.

He waved and then got into the car before she decided whether to wave back or not.

"Who is he, Daed?" She cringed, wishing she hadn't asked.

"I met him. He seems nice enough, but I don't remember his name or that of any of the other half-dozen young men I met today. Maybe John or Jacob? Lizzy will know."

"Don't you dare tell her I asked." She turned from the window and took the broom in hand. "I was just curious, and she'll pester me until I'm as wrung out as a desert."

Daed struck a match and lit another kerosene lantern. "Not a word from me." He shook the match and tossed it into the sink. "Has she gotten that bad?"

"Since spring. She's sure all sting in my life will disappear if I find someone new. The community's always pushed the singles, but she wasn't like that before Henry."

"We only want our young people to find someone."

"I know, but it's a little silly to say you trust God to find us a mate and then to pressure *us* to find one. Why is that?"

He shrugged. "We're a few bales shy of a wagonload, I guess."

She elbowed him. "Daed, what an awful thing to say about the rest of the community."

"Just about them? Watch it, Bethie girl. I'll leave here without boarding up that window." His smile reminded her of the steadiness of a good man, and loneliness swept through her.

While her Daed moved in and out of her apartment, going up and down the steps with materials to board up the window, she swept the floor several times, trying to make sense of her emotions. Her mind zipped with a hundred thoughts and her heart with too many feelings. How odd to see that man again.

But she had to stop thinking about him. Taking Jonah's letter in hand, she unfolded it again. At least she had a fascinating old man she could share her thoughts with.

DEAR BETH,

YOU ARE WELCOME FOR THE GIFT BOX. FOR A WHILE THE SLEIGH I CARVED ON IT TRIED TO HIDE FROM ME, PERHAPS BECAUSE MY FEELINGS TOWARD SLEIGHS ARE THE OPPOSITE OF YOURS. BUT I'M GLAD IT MEANT SOMETHING SPECIAL TO YOU.

I HOPE YOU'LL ALLOW ME ROOM TO SHARE MY OPINION WITHOUT SHUTTING ME OUT.

I THINK YOUR EFFORT TO KEEP FROM BURDENING OTHERS WITH YOUR PAIN IS ADMIRABLE. YOU CLEARLY HAVE A LOT OF STRENGTH. BUT YOU MUST BALANCE THAT DESIRE WITH WHAT YOU NEED FROM OTHERS. IT SOUNDS AS IF YOU'VE REQUIRED TOO MUCH OF YOURSELF. I ASK THAT YOU CONSIDER SHARING IT WITH YOUR FATHER OR BISHOP — SOMEONE WHO CAN DIRECT YOU TOWARD HEALING.

A SECRET SO HEAVY THAT YOU CAN DO NO MORE THAN REFERENCE IT VAGUELY, AS YOU DID IN YOUR

LETTER, IS TOO HEAVY TO BE CARRIED ALONE. BE CAUTIOUS
AND WISE WITH YOUR CHOICE OF WHO TO TALK TO, BUT
DON'T LET IT STAY INSIDE YOU FOR TOO LONG. IT'LL EAT
UP EVERYTHING GOOD AND GROW STRONGER AS YOU GROW
WEAKER. BUT WHEN YOU FACE IT THROUGH THE EYES OF
SOMEONE YOU TRUST, YOU WILL GROW STRONGER, AND IT
WILL WEAKEN.

YOUR FRIEND,
JONAH

She closed the letter, hoping he was wrong about her true self
growing weaker. She feared he wasn't. But he didn't understand. If he
did, he'd not suggest telling anyone. With her pen in hand, she began
a letter to him.

While waiting on the right words to come to her, she studied the
handcrafted gift he'd given her. As she ran her fingers over the beauti-
fully etched scenery, an idea energized her. She'd been thinking too
narrowly about how to sell his work. If her bishop wouldn't let her
sell the items but his bishop would, she needed to find another store
owner who Jonah could go through. She could find the right buyer
and negotiate the agreement, and then Jonah could work with the
buyer directly after that.

It wasn't the answer she wanted, but it was a beginning point.
After a while maybe Omar would change his mind.

"Bethie, I'm all done for now." Her Daed wiped his hands off on a dishtowel. "I'll order glass on Monday and should have you a new window by next weekend."

"Denki, Daed."

The flame of the lamp in her hand wavered, causing the shadows to dance as she followed her Daed down the steps. After telling him good night, she went to her office. She turned the knob on the lamp, giving the fire more wick, then pulled a file of sellers from a drawer and looked for the address and phone number of Gabe Price, a Plain Mennonite who owned a store. He not only bought a lot of Amish-made items from her, but he had great connections to other possible buyers and not just other stores. He also furnished items to a couple of resort owners. Since Gabe only lived an hour from Jonah, her plan for them to work together should be doable.

Surely it was time she pushed a little harder to get her way. She'd given Omar time to work through his reservations. He hadn't. If she made no profit in this plan, he had nothing to hold against her, did he? Jonah's work deserved to be made available to more people. She would call Gloria and go see Gabe Price as soon as she could. After all, if she hoped to talk Gabe into carrying Jonah's work, he needed to see the depth of the old man's skill. She couldn't show him that through a phone conversation.

The hour grew late, and she felt ready to crawl into bed. Although slipping into her nightgown and snuggling under the covers sounded appealing, she wasn't sleepy. She took the kerosene lantern with her and went upstairs.

She really wanted to write a long letter to Jonah. If he didn't want to read all she wrote, he could use the letter to start a fire. Or maybe she should buy a diary and leave the poor man alone.

"He's old, Beth, not bored silly," she mumbled to herself.

In the dimness of the barn, rays of daylight sifted through the cracks in the walls as Jonah studied the sleigh. The broken rig sat in this dreary place year in and year out. How could something as simple as a sleigh conjure dreams of happiness for one and nightmares of defeat for another?

He slid a hand into his pocket, feeling the letter he'd received yesterday. Through her words Beth had carried him to places he didn't want to go, and he wished she hadn't been so deep and personal. At the same time, her transparency made him long for more. She'd been so open, but now a paraphrase of a silly nursery rhyme circled around inside him, squawking like chimney swifts—All the king's horses, and all the king's men couldn't put Beth together again.

A shaft of light rested lifeless against the filthy sleigh. That awful night when Jonah was but fifteen replayed in his mind as it had a thousand times before. The midwinter weather had warmed a bit, but by the next morning the half-melted snow had turned to ice. Three of his sisters and two of his brothers sat packed inside the sleigh, the fastest horse they owned hitched to it. Amos drove, flying across the fields and passing Jonah as he chopped a fallen tree into firewood. Mamm and Daed wouldn't let Amos get on the road, so he drove up and down the long hill, causing the surrounding fields to ring with delight from their siblings.

After several trips Amos brought the rig to a stop, teasing Jonah because he hadn't wanted to ride. Even then Jonah hated the gliding feel of a sleigh. It lacked control, and he wanted no part of it. While Amos teased him, Jonah moved away from the patch of wood to the center of the open field, packed a tight snowball, and threw it at Amos, smacking him hard. Amos slapped the reins against the horse's back and yelled.

The horse headed straight for Jonah, but he laughed as he sidestepped and doubled back. Amos went up the long hill, turned the sleigh around, and charged after Jonah again. He brought the horse around too quickly, and the sleigh hit a patch of ice and swung out wide. The rigging snapped, breaking the connection between horse and sleigh. The horse bolted, jerking the reins from Amos's hands, and the sleigh hurtled down the slope, straight toward a twenty-foot ravine.

Everything became blurry after that, but Jonah remembered it'd been a long, bloody fight to make the sleigh change course and veer into a nearby snowy embankment. And when the struggle was over, only Jonah had sustained more than bumps and bruises.

He ran his hand over the leather seat of the sleigh. The memory had dulled over the years, yet the injury he'd sustained remained. When Beth learned the truth about his identity, would her sense of embarrassment be like a wound that never fully healed?

He'd finished his letter of explanation to her even before hers arrived, but it'd been impossible to place it in the mailbox. How did one hurl a heavy object, even a truthful one, at someone on purpose? In certain ways she radiated aloofness, but if he had any ability to read her, that wasn't who she was. She used her indifference to keep people—suitors, he believed—at bay. She had the breadth, height, and depth within her to connect.

He should have mailed his letter already. A jumble of confused reasons kept him from doing so, but mostly he wasn't ready for the letters to end.

He ran his hand over the sleigh. If it were in working order, it would have the power to bring joy—not to him, but to someone.

The sound of someone entering his wood shop drew his attention. His grandmother's soft voice called to him. "Jonah."

"Back here."

She walked toward him, a beam of light shining from the hand-crank flashlight she held. "Hi."

Since this shop was his haven from a family that stayed too close sometimes, she was one of the few who entered, and she didn't come often. She said nothing, and the sounds of the wind chimes filled the empty space between them.

"Did you need something, Mammi?"

"I just wanted to ask you to supper."

He didn't believe that was all she wanted, but he wouldn't call her on it. "Nah, I'm good. Thanks, though."

She shifted, and after a long pause she finally spoke again. "You've been too quiet for more than a week. I just wondered if you left your voice in Pennsylvania and if we could go back and get it."

He chuckled. "I've just been thinking. That's all."

"About the accident?"

"Not so much."

"I can't know how to pray if you stay hidden."

His grandmother's faith was different from anyone else's he knew. She paced the floors praying Scripture over her family. Before sunrise she whispered specific verses over each member. He'd been little when he first heard her pray for each grandchild's future spouse.

He reached into his pocket and felt the letter. Emotions swirled from deep within, like a whirlpool that led to unknown worlds. "I…I saw a young woman in August. Just for a minute but she stole every thought. I had no idea who she was. Then I saw her again in Pennsylvania."

His grandmother waited, studying him like she always had when something weighed on him.

He shrugged. "She wears black."

Her soft wrinkles bunched in the center of her forehead. "She's in mourning."

"Ya. But she's been mourning far longer than is traditional. Since the man wasn't her husband, it should have been over nearly a year ago."

"That's unusual."

"Beth is unusual. And I can't understand what it is about her that draws me. I'm tired of thinking about her, worrying about her, and yet if she slips my mind for a minute, I intentionally recall memories of her and her letters." He released his hold on the letter inside his pocket. "It's ridiculous. I don't know her well enough for all this nonsense. And what I do know makes the relationship impossible."

His grandmother climbed into the sleigh and sat. "I think it sounds like you found that treasured piece, the one you said you'd know when you saw it."

He'd felt the pull of Beth from the moment he saw her, but he believed he'd felt it long before then. It rested inside his faith during year after year of waiting.

But so much more separated them than the secrets Beth had shared because Lizzy had tricked her. He was convinced she wanted nothing to do with another man. Why else would she keep wearing black? And even if they worked through that, she provided much of the economic stability of her community. She didn't just live in Pennsylvania; her feet were cemented there.

Mammi angled her head. "Is she...who you want?"

"I'm not sure it matters what I want. You were right when you said I'm an idealist. I thought when I found the right person, we'd carve a life together, creating amazing scenes of things we'd both always wanted. I hate how I sound, so over the top with emotions, but I've waited so long, hoping I'd find her. And now everything is all wrong."

Mammi sighed. "If you can't carve the image you want, then carve what you can." She stepped out of the sleigh. "We take what is and trust that God is making things we can't yet see." She touched the place on his hand where his two missing fingers had once been. "You use pieces of wood most people would burn in a fireplace, and you make them into something only you can." She picked up his cane and passed it to him.

"Carve what can be carved." That idea sat really well with him. "You're pretty smart."

"So are you." She gave the flashlight a few hard cranks, making the beam of light grow stronger. "There's supper at our house if you're interested."

"Ya? Is it any good?"

"Better than your burnt toast specialty."

He started to leave but then paused and held the kerosene lantern near the sleigh. Between him and Beth, maybe he should be the first to refuse to hoard broken things from the past. If he could make himself renovate this sleigh, he might find it had more to give than bad memories and haunting voices.

Fourteen

Gabe Price walked beside Beth as they left his office. "How soon before you'll know?"

Beth's heart pounded with excitement, and she glanced at Gloria, who rose from her chair in the waiting room.

Beth kept her tone even, her emotions in check, as she put on her winter jacket. "I'll talk with Jonah Kinsinger as soon as I can reach him. He may need a while to think before responding, but I expect to have an answer for you within a week."

Gabe walked with her as they went to the van. The early-November air made her shiver.

He opened the door. "Sounds good. I hope this works out."

She slid into the vehicle. "Me too."

Gabe closed the door, and Gloria started the engine. Beth waved and managed to keep her excitement under control until they were out of his driveway.

"Yes!" Beth stomped her feet in quick succession. "Can you believe this? If Jonah agrees to these contracts, it'll be the best deal I've ever made for an Amish craftsman."

"I've always said you got confidence, Bethie girl. Bold, brassy gall. That's all I can say."

"Ya, but look what I came away with." She pulled the contracts out of her bag. "You know my next question, right?"

"Hmm, let me think about this. It'll have something to do with going to Jonah Kinsinger's place."

"If he had a phone, I'd call first, but even if we can't catch him at home, we can leave the information at Pete's. Maybe Pete can tell us where to find him."

"Who are you talking to? There's no way you're heading back to Pennsylvania without a face-to-face with Jonah, even if we have to stay at the closest motel and try again tomorrow."

"We've been traveling together for too long, Gloria. What else can you tell me about myself?"

"That you're not hungry, but I am. That you won't need a rest room for another four hours, but I do. That you probably slept no more than three hours last night getting ready for today, and on the way home you'll fall asleep. And that you pay well enough that I'm willing to drop everything almost anytime you need a driver."

Beth drummed her fingers on her canvas briefcase, ready to tell Gloria she knew about her longstanding agreement with Beth's parents. "Well, you have more incentive than just what I pay you, don't you?"

Gloria glanced from the road to Beth and back again several times. "You're not supposed to know about that."

"What, am I eighteen and on my first business trip again?"

"How long have you known?"

"Since I was eighteen and going on my second trip."

Gloria broke into laughter. "They love you, you know."

The joy of the deal faded, and she managed a nod. She knew. The problem was she'd kept so much of herself from them once she began having trouble with Henry that they no longer knew the real her. Even when in the room with them, she missed the closeness she'd once cherished.

"Your family couldn't stand letting you go on these trips without a chaperone."

"So they sweeten the pot because you're the safest driver they know, and you report back to them if I start some ungodly behavior like eating without a silent prayer before and after the meal, right?"

Gloria chuckled. "You have a dry sense of humor. Sometimes I don't know if you're teasing or perfectly serious. They trust me to keep you safe. That's all they really want."

"Well, then, let's safely travel to Jonah's place. You know where he lives?"

"I know. Do we need to call Lizzy and say we're extending the trip by a few hours?"

"I guess we do. I wasn't sure how this would go with Gabe, so I didn't tell her we might go on to Jonah's. You stop as needed for food and rest rooms. You call. You drive. I'll work."

Beth opened her briefcase and removed paperwork. The next time she looked up, they were passing through the little town of Tracing and were near Pete's Antiques. The roads twisted and curved until Gloria pulled into a driveway.

"That's the house Lizzy went to," Gloria said, pointing. "Then she went into that shop."

Beth slid the files and contracts into her briefcase. "I need to talk with Jonah alone, but you can't stay in the van the whole time. If he's home, I hope to be a while."

"Your aunt sure liked him. Sounds to me like he's good at working his way into the hearts of Hertzler women."

Beth opened the door. "You coming?"

"I'll wait here for now. We'll change plans as needed."

Driving the rig toward home, Jonah listened while Amos shared humorous stories from their day at the lumbermill business. The moment Jonah guided the horse and carriage into the driveway, he spotted a van. It looked like the same vehicle Lizzy had used when she visited, although there was no shortage of white work vans in these parts.

Before he could direct the horse to swing the buggy wide so he could see the license plate, his grandmother burst through the door and hurried down the steps. The intensity on her face caused him to stop the rig.

"Beth's here," she said. "Arrived about forty minutes ago."

He couldn't name the emotion that thundered through him—hope, unrest, anxiety—but his insides felt caught in a hailstorm. "Beth or Lizzy?"

"She's wearing black. That's Beth, right?"

He passed the reins to Amos. "Ya. Where is she?"

"Since I thought she was the one you told me about, I sent her to your place. Her driver is inside with me."

Without asking any of the questions he wanted to, he headed for his cabin. Cold air circled around him and dead November leaves crunched under his feet as he walked to his house. Smoke rose from his chimney, and he wondered if his grandfather had started a fire for her. If his *grossdaddi* had walked into Jonah's home, she already knew the man writing to her wasn't who she'd thought. He said a silent prayer and went inside.

Beth sat in a ladder back at the worktable in his living room, her attention on the carving in front of her. She held one of his many finished crossword magazines in her hand.

The moment she looked up, emotion drained from her face, and she reminded him of the stark beauty of tree limbs in winter.

He crossed the room. "Beth."

Her blue eyes reflected unease as she laid the magazine down. He removed his hat and set it on the table.

"I'm Jonah Kinsinger."

She stood. "What?" Disbelief colored her whisper.

"I have to tell you a few things that will be hard to hear at first, but I see no reason for us to end our friendship because I'm younger than you thought. It's still me, Beth. And the woman I've been getting to know is really you." He pointed to the carving. "I understand that you like my work."

"*Your* work?" She grabbed her satchel and pulled out one of his letters. "This Jonah Kinsinger?"

"Ya. There was a mix-up, and I didn't know I was writing to you, and you didn't know… Well, I realized something was wrong the night I called the store. Remember the odd conversation you had with—"

"What?" she interrupted, but he doubted she actually wanted any information repeated.

"It's not as bad as it sounds. I was shocked too when I learned of the misunderstanding."

Confusion, embarrassment, and horror were written on her face.

Pursing her lips, she cleared her throat. "Yes, well, I…uh." Her voice wavered, and she cleared her throat again. "I brought an offer for you to consider." She tossed his letter onto the table and reached into her satchel. "It seems"—she licked her lips and drew a deep breath—"that, uh, we have a man interested in your work."

"Beth, I'm sorry, but there's an explanation. Don't hide behind your work. Can we talk about this?"

With her eyes on the contracts in her hand, she held them out to him. "No, but thank you, anyway."

Her voice regained some evenness as she fought to remain calm. She'd shut him out. Professionalism stood in her stead. He could see feelings and thoughts running through her, but she refused to share any of them with him. He began to understand why Lizzy would resort to deception to circumvent her will.

Reluctant to point a finger at the person who had tricked them both, he tried again. "Miscommunication caused the letters to start."

"Not a problem. We have it all settled now, don't we?" While holding the contracts out to him with one hand, she covered her eyes with the other for a moment, visibly shaking. Then she lowered her hand. "Take a few days and look that over. The deal would be between you and Gabe Price. If you have any questions, you can call Lizzy. I can relay any information to her."

"Beth."

She looked him directly in the eyes, anger starting to outweigh the hurt and embarrassment. "Do not try to act like this was all a mistake. Clearly I'm still gullible at times—something that won't happen again, I promise that—but I'm not inexperienced when it comes to men and deceit."

Men and deceit?

Feeling as if she were on the brink of really talking to him, he cringed when he heard his front door open.

"Hey, Jonah."

Jonah didn't turn around. "Now's not a good time, Amos. Please close the door on your way out."

Beth raised an eyebrow, defiance clear as she sidestepped him. She grabbed her satchel and coat. "Hi." She smiled at Amos, one of those professional looks Jonah was learning to despise. "We were discussing some work, but we're through."

"No we're not." Jonah moved closer but remained to the side. He didn't want to block her, only to get her to look at him. "You have a right to be angry. Say what you're feeling, but don't act like it's no big deal. It's still me, Beth. I made the carvings. I answered your letters. I've been getting to know you."

"A deceived part of me and a part I would not have chosen to share if I had known the truth. Which of those do you request to bow to your will?" Her matter-of-fact tone struck him like a physical blow.

Speechless, he watched as she walked out the door.

Once past the threshold, she paused and faced him. "That's a good offer, the best I've ever negotiated. If you don't intend to accept the work, please don't leave Gabe Price hanging. He needs to know by next week. Can I trust you with that much?"

"You can trust me with anything."

She rolled her eyes, but he saw the threatening tears before she turned and went down the porch steps.

Amos blinked, looking too stunned to move. "Sorry. I didn't mean to interrupt."

"Your timing stinks. She was so close to…" He stopped. Nothing that had happened was Amos's fault.

"Close to what?"

"Screaming, yelling, being honest."

"If that's what you've been looking for all these years, you've got strange taste in women." Amos sighed. "Well. If you want to provoke her, go after her."

The sensible part of him wanted to let her go. She deserved time to adjust and let the weight of her response settle. But if he let her go, would they talk later, or would her freshly poured cement wall have hardened? Guessing the answer, he worked his way down the steps and across the yard, leaning heavily on his cane.

Beth stood at the foot of his grandmother's steps, telling her good-bye as the driver descended the stairs.

With dead leaves scattering as he walked, she had to hear the unique scrape of his cane as he approached, but she didn't turn around. He stopped right behind her.

"You're being guarded and evasive, and that has its place. But we'll both be better off if you'd share what you're thinking."

She spun toward him. "Don't do this," she whispered. "Haven't I suffered enough humiliation without you asking for more?"

"Just take a walk with me, and we'll talk."

"Oh, I've shared plenty with you already, thanks."

He stood within inches of her, but he wasn't sure he'd ever been farther from anyone in his life. "Beth, I know you're not intentionally being cold—"

"Cold?" Her voice showed the first hint of real desire to lose control, and she leaned in even closer. "A piece of advice—never underestimate how cold I can be."

Jonah leaned back as if slapped. "I guess I'm learning that."

"And now we're leaving."

"Beth, don't go like this. I went to the hayride…"

She shot him a look of bitterness. "I'm done."

"I'm not. Come on, Beth. I went to the hayride to figure out what was going on. When I had the chance to tell you, it felt wrong to blurt it out. I needed more time to explain everything."

"It would've taken you thirty seconds to say your name clearly."

"You seemed content enough not to know it. Why is that?"

"Fine. You're completely in the right, and I'm completely in the wrong. I'll send no more letters, and I'll receive no more from you. Is that clear?" Her poised indifference was unsettling. "Gloria, please unlock the van door."

"You can hide behind black for the rest of your life." He stayed in step with her as she moved to the vehicle. "Others may not see what you're hiding, but you have to look into that darkness every day."

The anger and fight drained from her, and he didn't know how to move her in the opposite direction.

Without so much as a glance, she got into the van.

Fifteen

Gloria kept her eyes on the road and asked nothing as Beth sobbed. As the miles passed, her embarrassment faded, and memories of the night Henry died began to haunt her. She'd been so stubborn, so unkind. He'd begged for another chance, promises flowed from his lips, but she fought herself free and left—never to see him alive again.

"Gloria, go back."

Her eyes were large. "You sure?"

"Yes." But how could she face Jonah? He'd tricked her, and he knew too much. "No...keep going."

Visions of holding Henry's soaked, cold body against her own and her desperation for the nightmare to end engulfed her. She couldn't carry the weight of leaving like this. Not again.

"Go back."

Gloria glanced from the road to her but slowed the van. Soon they were in the Kinsinger driveway again.

"I don't know how long I'll be," Beth said. "I need to find peace between him and me before I can go."

Gloria pulled the vehicle directly in front of Jonah's place this time instead of his grandmother's. "I'll wait here."

"Denki."

"You're welcome."

Beth got out, but before she closed the door, Gloria called to her. Beth bent to look through the window.

"Are you sure he's safe?" she asked.

Thinking someone should have asked that question about Henry, Beth nodded. "I'm sure of it."

She moved to the front door and knocked.

"Kumm," Jonah's voice called.

Easing inside, she spotted him at the kitchen sink, his back to her as he filled the percolator with water.

"I'm fine." His voice filled the room with warmth. "I'm not hungry right now, but thanks. And I told you she was unusual. I know I shouldn't have pursued her when she was so mad, so don't even say it." He turned slightly and glanced toward the door. All of his movements stopped.

"Unusual?" She tried smiling but couldn't manage it. He knew so much about her. She felt as though she stood before him without her hair pulled under her prayer Kapp. "Is that the Ohio Amish way of saying 'troubled'?"

It was his turn to be startled. "I can't believe you came back. Did you leave something?"

She shook her head, all her words lost for a moment, and watched him set the coffeepot on the stove and light a flame under it.

His movements were as tranquil as crystal water flowing down a lazy stream. His back and shoulders looked strong, and she could envision him fighting the terrain and elements to pull that log out. She wondered if he was the man he appeared to be, the man he sounded like in his letters. She knew most men weren't like Henry, but she'd been attracted to him when they began their relationship, and she didn't know if she could trust the power of what she felt for Jonah.

She smoothed her apron. "You don't seem bothered by the clash we had, so if you're okay with things between us, I probably should head on home. I just… I was worried, but…you're fine. I'm fine."

He smiled. "Up to you, but I make really great coffee."

"I can't be here that long."

"Man, what is it about my coffee that makes everyone feel that way?"

The emptiness inside her eased a bit. He knew part of her secret, and she hadn't been destroyed by it. "Jonah, I came back because I need us to end peacefully, okay?"

"I admire that, Beth, and I understand. But I see no reason for our friendship to end, even if peacefully."

Her skin tingled from the awkwardness she felt. "There's no chance you didn't get my last letter, is there?"

He slung a dishtowel across his shoulder and shook his head. "I got it."

She shuddered. "Great."

Why did I share so much? From now on she had to do a better job of controlling and hiding her loneliness.

A tender smile crossed his face as he pulled two mugs from the cabinet. "So you thought I was cute, huh?"

Mortified, heat rushed through her body. Of the many things she'd written about, describing the reaction she'd had when she saw the nameless man at Pete's Antiques might have been the most frivolous. Then, like a teenager with a first crush, she'd expounded in her letter on the impression "the stranger" left on her when he came to Lizzy's supper and hayride event. "Well...not so much anymore."

His laughter eased the tension between them, and even with her lingering embarrassment, she knew she'd done the right thing in coming back. The aroma of coffee began to permeate the room, making the place feel warm and welcoming.

"How'd the mix-up happen?" she asked, already knowing the answer. Lizzy was the linchpin between them since her visit. She had to be in the center of it all.

He shook his head and said nothing. Leaning back against the counter, he set his cane next to him. For the first time she noticed he was missing two fingers. He had an appealing ruggedness about him, a presence that pulled on her. When she lifted her eyes, he seemed to look straight into her soul. She couldn't imagine what he must think of her.

He looked from her to his hand. "A sleighing accident."

She nodded. "The reason we have opposite feelings toward sleigh rides."

"That'd be it. At first I was a self-conscious teen who tried to hide my hand. As time passed, I realized everyone is damaged in one way or another."

"Some of us more than others." She lowered her eyes to the countertop, unable to look him in the eye. "And we all have to learn to get by with the limitations we're left with."

"That's only partially true, Beth. When I was injured physically, I went through surgeries and physical therapy. All of it was painful, but if I'd refused to have the operations and hadn't fought to regain use of my leg and arm, I'd be in constant pain and truly crippled, not just reliant on a cane."

She tried to comprehend, but her divided emotions still battled inside her. His pain was different from hers. But what she did understand slipped past her barriers and felt like a soothing balm on a painful burn. Maybe there was freedom to be found, even for her. Had she allowed her injury to do more damage to her than it should have?

The answer scraped away the freshly applied salve. When it came to Henry's death, she was no innocent casualty.

"I…I'm glad you got the help you needed, Jonah." She wanted to shake his hand, thank him for being gracious, and leave, but she couldn't make herself budge.

"Beth, healing isn't some special gift designed just for me."

His gentle warmth felt hauntingly familiar. He clutched his cane, went to the stove, and turned off the eye under the coffeepot. It seemed no time had passed since she'd walked back into his home, but since the coffee had finished percolating, she realized they must have been talking for fifteen minutes or more.

Jonah turned back to her. "In that sleighing incident…I was the only one who got physically hurt. But for a long time, my siblings suffered emotional trauma because of my injuries. It's been thirteen years since the accident. Shame or regret still crops up in Amos or one of the others. We talk it out, get some perspective, apply fresh forgiveness where needed, and keep moving on."

His words made her ache for that kind of openness with someone. When she thought she was coming to see the old man she'd been writing to, she'd planned to tell him about the night Henry died—not all of it, but maybe enough to lift some of the weight. Easing the solitude of her secret might help, even if she knew a pardon didn't exist for her. "For everything you know about me, there's much, much more that you don't."

"Beth." His gentle voice circulated through her blood, reminding her of a hundred dreams she once imagined for her life. "That day at Pete's, when we saw each other, I felt it too. I've thought of you so many times since then. Are you going to close me out because I don't know you when you're the one not giving me that chance?"

She went to the kitchen table and picked up the letter she'd tossed there earlier. She always carried letters with her when traveling, an old habit in case she needed to reference some information or address a question. But in Jonah's case, she'd kept them with her because she enjoyed rereading them. Walking back to where he stood, she pulled it out of its envelope and opened it. "Did you mark out this line?"

He took the letter from her, studied it for a few moments, and then laid it on the counter in front of her. Without giving an answer, he opened two small tin canisters, added a spoon to each, and slid them her way. One contained sugar and the other powdered cream. "You're changing the subject. We were talking about you, about us."

She picked up the letter and lightly shook it. "You want honesty from me, but you can't give it?"

He took two mugs from the cabinet and moved to the stove. "Your aunt knew we needed each other's friendship. She saw that in both of us, but we agree she went about it completely wrong." He held out a mug of steaming coffee to her.

She didn't take it. Instead she nudged the letter toward him again. "What did the line she marked out say?"

He set the cup on the counter in front of her. "I think it said that your voice on paper sounded much different than you sounded in person. I noticed it in the first letter from you, but I thought maybe that's why you asked for us to write."

Beth's throat ached from the effort of bottling emotions she didn't want. Without meeting her, Jonah sensed more of who she was from a letter than others she had known since childhood did. Tears choked her, and she wished she hadn't asked about the marked-out line. "I should go."

He met her eyes but said nothing for a moment. She felt so transparent and couldn't sort out if it thrilled her or frightened her.

"I understand. You know what I'd like, but it's ultimately your choice." The finality in his voice dug deeper into the canyon of doubt inside her. He took a sip of his drink. "I'll miss hearing from you, Beth."

She stared at the black liquid in her cup, not wanting to see the message in his face again. "If you were an old man, I'd be a nice girl to write to, one who could help you earn money selling your carvings.

But you're not old, and I can't chance what might happen if I don't walk away. There are boundaries I can't cross."

"That's how you've been coping, I know, but I don't believe that's who you want to be."

A sob escaped her, and she turned her back to him. To her right stood a set of french doors, framing a view of rolling pastures, sprawling oaks, and a huge moon, highlighting the work of a God larger than her pain. "I felt drawn to a man once before." She whispered, but she knew by Jonah's silence that he'd heard her. "Only a little compared to…us. But it dug two graves—his and mine."

Jonah stepped closer. "Can you tell me what happened?"

She'd come this far. "There were two Henry Smuckers. The one I agreed to marry and the one who showed up soon after I said yes to his proposal. The latter came out of hiding whenever he didn't like something."

It was several minutes before she could say more, but Jonah waited.

"The longer we were engaged, the more things Henry didn't like about my life. He wanted to control my every thought, every feeling. Accused me of caring too much for my family. He especially resented my feelings for Lizzy and my Daed. He demanded I give up the store. At first I avoided family gatherings, worked fewer hours—anything that might make him feel more at ease. No matter what I changed for him, it wasn't enough. His complaining turned into yelling. Then he started getting rough with me—nothing huge, just quiet ways of leaving bruises on my arms. A day or two later he'd be the Henry I fell for…warm, endearing, funny. He said he knew he needed to change, and if I'd help him, he would. But the closer we got to our wedding, the worse he became. I could see only misery ahead. I wanted to remain loyal, but I couldn't marry him. I grew more distant, indifferent, and when I no longer cared whether he needed me or if I was being selfish, I told him I was done. And I didn't care what it did to him."

She turned to face Jonah and drew a deep breath. "He wasn't from Apple Ridge, but he was staying with one of his uncles when I went to see him. It had been pouring rain for days. We stood on the porch, and I told him I couldn't marry him. At first he was kind and understanding, trying to convince me to change my mind. Then he grew angry and began threatening me. He lifted me off my feet and banged my back against the side of the house, demanding"—she looked Jonah straight in the eye—"*demanding* I marry him. I broke free and ran for my buggy. He chased me, begging me not to leave him, swearing he'd change. But I told him it was too late. He threatened to spread lies, said he'd break my Daed's heart and ruin my business and…" She wiped a tear from her cheek. "Suddenly I could see that his problems were deeper than insecurity and uncontrollable anger. He needed real help, but I just wanted out. As I climbed into the buggy, he…he jerked me out and then dropped me. I slid through the muck in the yard. When he grabbed me off the ground, I kicked and lashed out with all my strength. I…I guess I caught him off guard, because he went down to his knees in pain." She rubbed her eyes. "Dear God, forgive me. While he was still down, I said horrid things one person should never say to another." She closed her eyes. "And while he screamed promises from the mud, I left."

"And Henry?"

"The next day he was found downstream—dead, drowned. Before daylight his uncle brought me the news, and I went to where they'd found him. I knelt in the rain, holding him, with no way to change the past. The muddy, frothy water roaring nearby was unusually powerful from the previous days of rain. When the police arrived, I told them about our fight. One of the officers said they'd need to investigate but that I should protect Henry's family and my own by keeping the argument and the breakup to myself. It didn't take long for them to verify that Henry was still alive when I left him and that I was home when he came up missing. Another officer, a detective, I think, said he'd found a spot on the creek bank where it looked as if it had caved under Henry's feet. There were claw marks in the mud nearby that showed where Henry had tried to get ashore, so they didn't believe foul play or suicide was the cause. But they told me again that it wouldn't help anyone to share what Henry was really like or the hurt he was feeling when he died. I understood it would hurt everyone I loved to learn the truth. And I kept thinking if I'd been more loyal, been the kind of person who'd stand by my fiancé no matter what, then he wouldn't be dead."

"Beth, you're blaming you for protecting yourself. Can't you see that?"

"I should have seen his problems sooner. When his issues were serious, I should have been strong enough to help him. But as I stood at Henry's grave site the day he was buried, covered in bruises no one would ever see, I knew it didn't matter what I should have done, only what I would do. Make sure never to let it happen again."

"You question your loyalty, but didn't his proposal come with an unspoken promise of love and protection?"

She didn't answer. The logical part of her understood that, but the hardness that she felt inside didn't yield to reason. "None of that matters now. I try to do what's right. Try to respond to those around me like before Henry's death, but it's not the same."

He dumped a spoonful of sugar and one of powered cream into a mug. "And ever since, you hide from your future behind black." He stirred the coffee. "Henry had problems, the kind we almost never hear of among the Amish. But you did the right thing not marrying him." He walked to where she stood and held out the mug to her. "The right thing, Beth."

"How could it be right if I carry Henry's blood on my hands?"

"The only blood on you—whether his or yours—is what he spilled every time he hurt you."

His words sliced through the lies she couldn't find freedom from, leaving her staggering at the revelation that someone else knew her secret—and didn't find her guilty. "I…I need to go."

"Then take a few sips while I get something I want you to have."

She took the cup. Her chest ached from the tears, but she was glad to have finally told someone. She drew the warm mug to her lips and drank. The flavor was both customary and keenly rare.

Like the man himself.

Breathing in the aroma, she couldn't imagine what he'd used or done differently to make it so delicious.

He came back into the room with a letter in hand. "It's the one I wrote to you after I came to the hayride. I mean every word, if you can manage to hear it."

She kept both hands wrapped around her mug. "No more, Jonah. It's too much, and I can't take it. Lizzy shouldn't have thrown us together. I just gave you every reason you need to let me go." She held the drink out to him.

He took the cup, but with his index and middle finger of that same hand, he continued to hold the letter out to her. "Take the letter. Mostly it says what I've already said here today, but you'll be able to hear it better when you've had more time to adjust to who you've really been writing to. Just tell me you'll read it, and I'll let you be. I hope to hear from you, though."

"You won't."

In spite of her assurance, she eased the letter from his fingers before she turned and left.

Sixteen

*B*eth and Gloria rode home in silence, the joy of the business deal gone. Despite Beth's anger with Lizzy, Jonah's voice continued to work its way through her, as if they stood in the same room. His letter tormented her, begging to be read, but she left it sealed.

After one stop for food and gas, they continued on. She hadn't eaten, and between pondering what Jonah had said and thinking about how ridiculously wrong Lizzy was to have pulled such a stunt, she couldn't manage to hold a conversation with Gloria.

The hum of the tires against the pavement continued mile after mile, and her emotions finally began to settle. The lull of the van slowly overtook Beth's anxiety, and she grew drowsy. As sleep eased over her, sleigh bells rang, and children's laughter echoed. Darkness filled every corner of where she stood. It matched her clothing. It matched who she'd become, and she couldn't see a way out. The tinkling sound of bells and laughter came from a place ahead of her.

Feeling her way through the darkness, she walked and walked. Her palms bumped against a heavy wooden door, but it swung open easily, and she stepped onto a snow-covered field. The moon glistened on the white backdrop. A man appeared in front of her. A beautiful sleigh held several children of various ages—how many she couldn't tell. The man's hand stretched toward her, but she refused. He motioned for her, unable to cross some unseen barrier.

She knew this place. Fear jolted through her.

Demanding her body to wake, she slowly became aware of the car seat beneath her, but the sound of sleigh bells continued. Willing herself to breathe deeply and become fully conscious, she seemed to be awake several long moments before the jingling faded.

Beth sat up, watching the silhouettes of night pass by until Gloria pulled into Lizzy's driveway. Even though it was past midnight, going to her aunt's house after a trip was the routine, one Beth couldn't avoid or Lizzy would come to her. That would be especially true since Gloria had called Lizzy after they'd left Gabe's to say they were going to Jonah Kinsinger's.

Beth wished she knew how to share the mix of anger and humiliation circling inside her, plus the confusing situation Lizzy had heaped on her.

Gloria stopped the van.

Beth gathered her things. "I don't know what all you report back to Daed, but this situation with Jonah is personal, and I'm twenty-six."

"One day I'd like to understand how you had such a row with a man you'd never met before, two of 'em, in fact, but I won't say a word to anyone." Gloria looked at her. "You okay?"

"I'm not sure," Beth mumbled, wishing she knew the answer. "Do you believe people need surgery and physical therapy for emotional or soul wounds?"

Gloria put the van in Park. "I never thought about it in those terms, but, yeah, I do."

"Jonah believes it. He thinks if I'd quit trying to hide long enough to face what's killing me, I might find happiness again." Beth paused. "If you held a secret, an awful one that would hurt everybody, would you tell your family or pastor?"

Gloria ran her palm back and forth over the steering wheel. "I've known you for a long time, and I don't want to say anything that would hurt you, but the truth is, if a secret was doing to me what it's done to you, I'd tell. I guess you should ask yourself if holding on to the secret isn't hurting people just as badly as telling them the truth."

Beth had thought she was sparing her family, Lizzy in particular. "Go on. I'm listening."

"Isn't it the same amount of pain either way? Only you're doling it out little by little over a lifetime and allowing it into the future as well as the past." Gloria pushed a button, turning on an overhead light. "How long will you punish yourself?"

"I don't know. I can't see ever getting past it, really."

"Then why did Christ die?"

Gloria's words hit hard, and Beth wondered if somehow the answer she needed rested in that simple question. "I've asked Him to forgive me."

"With a tender spirit like yours, I'm sure that part came naturally. But if you continue to carry the guilt, it's like what He did is not sufficient. As if you're telling God that His gift of mercy is not powerful enough to help *you* forgive you."

"But I…" Beth fidgeted with the canvas carryall, unsure what word to use to complete the sentence.

"Sinned? Blew it? Made a stupid mistake? Did something you can't undo? It's all covered."

It's covered.

The words entered Beth, echoing over and over again. She ached to be free of her past, but that wasn't going to happen. Could she at least stop hating herself over it?

She whispered a thank-you to Gloria and got out of the van. Lizzy stood on the porch, watching as Beth climbed the steps. With no words to express her feelings, Beth went inside without speaking.

Lizzy closed the door behind them. The large open space of the kitchen and sitting area was warm and inviting. The fireplace roared with flames, and the air carried the aroma of stew and cornbread. Sometimes Beth didn't know if Lizzy was her mother, aunt, sister, or best friend. In one way or another, she was each of those.

"I'm sorry, Beth."

Beth turned and faced her aunt. "I don't even know what to say. You had no right. But you knew that when you began this."

Lines of regret creased Lizzy's face. "I…I just wanted to help, but Jonah's right—I was wrong to trick you. Once I started, I couldn't make myself tell you."

Beth threw her satchel onto the couch. "What you did was so much more cruel than just leaving me alone. I wrote personal things to him, Lizzy. The kind of stuff I'd never have told someone his age. Then I showed up at his place with no clue what I was walking into. Why would you do that to me?"

"I'm so sorry."

"No." Beth peeled off her jacket and tossed it across the arm of a chair. "The question is why, Lizzy. Not how do you feel about it."

Lizzy's hands had an almost undetectable tremble as she gestured toward Beth. "You liked his work, and—"

Beth stepped forward and placed her index finger against her aunt's lips, shushing her. "Why?"

Lizzy's eyes filled with tears. "Because I was scared for you. You wouldn't let me inside that dark place where you hide, and you refused to step outside of it. Because you think you want to be alone the rest of your life, and you don't know what it's like. Jonah's work was the first thing to interest you in such a long time, and I grabbed on to it." Lizzy broke into tears. "Because I thought he might make you feel something again, and I feared for your future more than I feared your anger."

The weight of Lizzy's worries settled over Beth, and her aunt's emotions tangled into so many of her own. Beth's fears began when she realized the lines between trust and distrust, love and apathy, controlled anger and meanness were so thin a person could cross over with no effort at all.

Feeling weary, she moved to the sofa. Lizzy melted into a nearby chair, and neither one spoke. The dancing flames in the hearth slowly faded, leaving mostly embers in their stead.

Beth reached for Lizzy's hand. "I forgive you, Lizzy." She squeezed gently before letting go. "And I understand making poor choices and keeping secrets. Besides, I can't honestly blame you. I've been a mess for so long."

"You're just a little lost. Losing Henry was powerful hard on you. You'll find love again. I know you will."

"Lizzy…" Beth's chest ached with the truth. "I wasn't in love with Henry, not by the time of the accident. We had quite a brawl about it hours before he died."

Her aunt's eyes filled with shock and tears, but she remained outwardly calm. Beth had no doubt Lizzy would weep over the news when she let herself. Beth should have never tried to protect everyone. If she hadn't, most of the pain of her failed relationship with Henry would be behind them.

"I'm taking off work tomorrow. I need to tell Daed and Omar things I should have told them long ago."

A box of Christmas crafts sat on the other end of the couch. Beth moved the container to the floor, took off her shoes, and stretched out. She was worn out and should have gone home to sleep, but she and Lizzy needed each other tonight. "You didn't start making Christmas cards as you planned."

Lizzy shrugged. "After Gloria called, I wasn't in the mood to be creative. I still have six weeks to get them made and delivered."

Beth released a sigh she'd been holding since before Henry died. "I haven't seen or felt Christmas in years. Sometimes it doesn't feel like it will ever come again."

Lizzy covered her with a blanket and sat on the coffee table next to her. "You'll start enjoying Christmas again. I know it. Just look at the steps you're taking."

"It's taken me too long, and yet it's not been nearly long enough."

"You weren't ready sooner. But it has been long enough." Lizzy took the straight pins out of Beth's prayer Kapp and lifted it from her head. "How did things go between you and Jonah?"

"Embarrassing. Awful. Awkward." Beth closed her eyes and yawned. "Lizzy?"

Her aunt kissed her forehead. "Ya?"

Sleep pulled on her. "I don't want to wear black anymore."

"I'll loan you anything you want while we make you new clothes."

"I love you," Beth mumbled as sleep took over. Even as sleigh bells began to jingle in her awaiting dream, she felt Lizzy tuck the blanket around her.

"I know you do."

Seventeen

*I*nside Lizzy's home Beth watched her family, awed at the power of love. The kitchen table had been extended to make room for the whole family. Sunday afternoon conversations ran like threads through a homemade dress, each one helping to hold the family together. Her mother glanced at her and winked while feeding a grandbaby a spoonful of applesauce.

Beth's Daed placed a piece of pie in front of her and sat on the bench seat beside her. "How'd we do?"

She ran her fork through the butternut squash pie and took a bite. "My part is perfect. Yours...not so much."

"But we blended our ingredients, Bethie girl."

"And mine is perfect."

He chuckled. "Then I guess my part isn't good enough for me to help you make desserts later this week for our Thanksgiving meal."

"Oh, no. As a new cook, you have to help." She squelched a giggle and leaned her shoulder into his. "You need the practice."

Two weeks ago she had sat down with him and the bishop and

told them everything. It'd been the first time she'd seen tears in her father's eyes. Since that day Beth and her family had been taking the first steps on a journey to find healing.

Not long after meeting with Omar and her Daed, she'd returned to Henry's grave one last time, a severing of ties of sorts. She'd gone there so many times since he'd died, not out of love and only partially out of guilt. Like so many other things, her reason for going was clearer now. During each visit she'd woven a rope that kept her tied to that cemetery.

Whether intentional or not, Henry had begun a cycle of fear—fear of displeasing him and fear of his anger. Before the breakup she'd been anxious over ending the relationship and fearful of what he'd do, fearful of what their families and the community would think of her. Oddly, his death hadn't stopped what he'd begun. Before she'd worn her first black dress, fear had splintered into a hundred pieces inside her, and each one turned into a painful ulcer. To keep anyone from touching those spots, she'd pulled away before they got a chance.

Now, she understood, that was her past. Today she was new, with hope and promise for tomorrow. She wanted to stop fear from ruling her. She'd begun that process, but she imagined it would take a while to find all the places where splinters still hid.

The only thing truly missing from her life was the pleasure of writing to Jonah. She might write him one day, but she needed to sort through her thoughts, problems, and emotions on her own first. She was rebuilding herself—a better self.

Her rebuilding work wasn't the only thing keeping her from writing to him. Since he'd been pulled into her life through trickery, she hesitated to reach out to him. Still, she should touch base with him. She might discover that he was waiting for her to contact him as he'd said before she left his home, or she might find that after he thought everything over, he'd changed his mind about her.

There was only one way to find out.

Jonah finished applying another coat of lacquer to the sleigh, then set the brush in a can of turpentine. He'd realized he'd been doing the same thing with the sleigh that Beth had been doing by wearing black—not letting go of the past nor truly entering the future.

In spite of all the work he'd done to the sleigh, including taking it to the blacksmith's and having the runners reworked, it wasn't finished yet. But it would be, and he'd give it to Beth as a Christmas present. He hadn't yet figured out how he'd get it there. Even if the snow was perfect and he were willing to drive it, which he wasn't, it couldn't be driven all the way to Apple Ridge, Pennsylvania. But he still had time to figure it out. With each new coat of paint or lacquer, he prayed for Beth.

He walked to the mailbox, hoping the carrier had already run. Four weeks had passed without a word from her, but he kept checking. He'd asked that none of his family get his mail for him. Otherwise, after he checked the box, he had to check with his sister-in-law and grandmother to see if either of them had picked up his mail. Until Beth, he appreciated them bringing the mail in.

The dreary early-December sky spat the first sleet of the season. It wouldn't amount to much, not right after Thanksgiving like this. He'd been using his time to help at his family's lumberyard, to work on the sleigh, and to fill orders for Gabe. It felt good and right to use his carving skills again, but he had questions for Beth, legitimate business ones, and he couldn't call her. He'd told her he wouldn't reach out, and he wouldn't. She had to make the first move. If his grandmother's prayers were as powerful as he believed, and if Beth was truly the one for him, as he believed, then he'd just have to wait.

He opened his mailbox, seeing a couple of envelopes stuck between junk mail advertisements. Closing the box with his elbow, he flipped through the letters. Energy shot through him at the sight of Beth's handwriting. He tore the envelope open.

Dear Jonah,

I hope this letter finds you well. I'm holding my own, having gone through—as you call them—several surgeries. The physical therapy isn't nearly as bad as I thought. My Daed and I have had a lot of long talks. Omar, our bishop, is a kind and gentle man, who comes by my office two afternoons a week. He was one of Henry's uncles here in Apple Ridge. He thought he'd seen shadows of Henry's darker side, but he kept hoping he was mistaken.

Omar's counsel and understanding have been deep and helpful. I carry my past with a sense of peace and faith in God's mercy toward both Henry and myself.

How you stepped into my darkness, bringing a light no one else could, I'll never know. But I want to thank you.

I spoke with Gabe, who said he talked to you last week but that you had a few questions he couldn't answer. Please feel free to call the store at any time.

Gratefully yours,
Beth

As pleased as he was for permission to contact her, she sounded formal and professional. He should expect no less, he supposed. She'd been as injured in her relationship with Henry as Jonah had in the sleigh accident, only his injuries had not been hidden nor left to fester. Teams of skilled professionals, along with his family, openly addressed each issue month after month, year after year, until he was as healed as he'd ever get.

Sliding the letter into his pants pocket, Jonah walked toward the barn. This was what he'd been hoping for, an invitation to call her. He saddled his horse and headed for Pete's. After arriving he talked with his friend briefly, then lifted the receiver to call Beth. As he dialed her number, hope worked its way through him.

"Hertzlers' Dry Goods."

Her voice moved into the empty spaces of the last few weeks, filling him with contentment. "Hi, Beth. This is Jonah."

"Hello, Jonah." The sound of papers being shuffled came through the phone. "What can I do for you today?"

Not treat him like a client would be a start, but after she'd revealed her pain to him, he understood her defenses. She wasn't in the same place he was. He knew what he wanted from this relationship. He'd waited so long for her. Years.

"You said I could contact you with any questions, and I have a good many."

"You received my letter already?"

Deciding how much restraint to use, he leaned one forearm on the counter next to the cash register. "I've had it all of thirty minutes."

She chuckled. "If I were your boss, I'd be furious at such a delay."

He heard more warmth in her voice and felt confident that open honesty without pressuring her was welcome. "I needed time to saddle a horse and get to Pete's. Not all of us have a phone on our desk... or even in our barn."

"Get a faster horse."

The touch of banter held the promise of all he knew they could be in time. "I like the horse I have, thank you."

"I knew the contracts would be confusing. They're written as separate agreements so you can choose which requests you wish to fill."

Sensing that he should stick to business for now, he asked a few questions, and she answered. When he felt a nudge inside him to shift the conversation, he changed the topic. "So how are you doing, Beth?"

"Me? That's been the topic of conversation too much lately. I even wrote you a letter about all the me stuff."

"Yes you did, and I'm very thankful for that. So then tell me about your Thanksgiving and what's happening with your store."

She didn't respond, and he wondered which she'd do—remain professionally distant or share some small part of herself with him. Either way they were making progress.

"Thanksgiving was really good. I think it's the first time I've tasted a meal in ages." She paused, possibly giving him a chance to talk, but he waited. "It feels like I've missed joy for far too long." She drew a slow breath. "Mamm and Daed and I talked for hours. My Daed helped me make his favorite dessert. It seemed so odd to have a man in the kitchen actually cooking, but it healed something inside both of us. It's crazy at the store right now, and it will be like running a race until we close at noon on Christmas Eve. How about you?"

"The actual work in the lumberyard itself is slow this time of year, but pricing jobs to clear timber off of land is fairly busy. People need money to get through the winter months, and we pay in advance. I had the best Thanksgiving I've had in a very long time." He paused, wondering if he should say what he wanted. He decided it might not be wise but to chance it anyway. "My family—they're all great. But this Thanksgiving had a new hope…concerning us."

She grew quiet again. "Ya, I…I felt those hopes too."

Her quiet, restrained confession made him feel much like he had when he'd started building his cabin—full of promise but no strength against the elements just yet.

"About those contracts, Jonah." She veered the conversation back to business. "Do you understand the requests concerning each cabin? The construction will take place in phases. The first phase includes the twenty cabins they want ready for occupants by May first."

"Gabe wants me to carve on the back of chairs, the mantels, free-standing objects, cabinets, and something called Aeolian chimes."

"Aeolian chimes are the same as wind chimes. The owners of the resort know Gabe, and they're asking if you'll do these things. You're not obligated to do any more than you want, but the price they're willing to pay is incredible. I have Amish craftsmen making the cabinets, tables, chairs. That part of the deal will work out whether you choose to carve designs on them or not. Your first job is to choose what you're willing to carve, but once you decide, it has to be done for each cabin. The owners' top choice is for you to do the backs of the chairs, the cabinet doors, and the mantels to match. They're going for an upscale rustic look. It'll be beautiful. They'd like to pick a base color for the fabric used in each cabin for things like kitchen chair cushions, couches, and throw pillows. I didn't know if the color the interior decorator chose might affect what scenery you'd carve or not."

"I don't know either. I've never thought about it."

"Well, there are a couple of ways we can work this. You can create the carvings, and the interior decorator can choose a color that coordinates with whatever scenery you chose, or you can choose a color from a scheme first. I wrote the contracts so you had the freedom of choice, not the decorator."

"What's your favorite color, Beth?"

"It's not black, okay?"

"Better than okay. So what is it, and why?"

The conversation unwound like a spool of thread, magically sewing pieces of their lives together in the process. As the hours passed, she occasionally put him on hold while she tended to store business.

He didn't want to end the conversation, so he waited. Although most Amish avoided phones except for business, no one would object to their talking like this.

Each time she came back on the line, they seemed to be in a better place than before. He could hear people come into her office and ask questions. When she left the office a couple of times to help, with each beat, each movement, he understood more of who she was.

The physical distance between their two lives still nagged at him. Her roots were deeply planted in Apple Ridge. The community relied on her, and she adored her family and her work. He was part of a family-owned business that had been passed down for generations, and he was needed. Jonah, three of his brothers, and his Daed each had a specific job, and it took all of them to keep the mill profitable. He'd built more than just his dream cabin on acreage his grandfather had given him—on the very spot Jonah cherished most of all. He'd made a home for himself.

By the time he and Beth hung up, Jonah realized that for all they'd worked through to get to this point, they still faced a huge issue. He needed a solution.

It had been dark for hours when he finally walked into Pete's kitchen.

"I guess if you stay on the phone long enough, I gotta cook the meal." Pete chuckled and pointed to the plate of food on the back of the stove.

Jonah turned a chair around and straddled it. "I got a problem, Pete."

"Women'll do that to a man." The old bachelor winked.

Forty years ago Pete had come close to marrying, but for reasons he wouldn't talk about, it never took place. He grabbed the plate of food and a fork and set it in front of Jonah.

Jonah took a bite of mashed potatoes. "Ya, but this one's worth it."

"Well, you know what I always say about problems."

"Start at desire and work from there."

"Yep. So bottom line, no fantasy nonsense, what do you want?"

"Beth Hertzler to be my wife." As soon as he said it, he got a bad feeling in his gut. "Scratch that. I'd like to be the husband of Beth Hertzler."

"Don't see the difference."

"In one scenario she's mine. In the other I'm hers."

"Still lost here."

"You'll have to trust me. I think I know the solution. Thanks."

Pete scratched his head, looking confused. "Anytime. Are you gonna tell me?"

"I need to move to Pennsylvania and be her husband, not have her move here to be my wife."

"That's a lot to give up for a woman. I don't recommend it."

Jonah shrugged. "If she'll have me, my mind's made up. I just don't know how I'll leave the business."

Eighteen

Beth held the phone to her ear, feeling the customary war between caution and desire. Silence lay between her and Jonah like newly fallen snow, and she struggled to find the right words. Her store closed Thursday at noon for Christmas Eve, and Jonah wanted to see her.

Part of her longed to go to Ohio and spend time with him as he'd asked. The rest of her wanted to slow everything down to a pace she didn't find so scary—something more like the laziness of sunset in midsummer rather than nightfall in winter.

Over the last three weeks he'd sent long, deeply moving letters, and he'd called her most evenings after the store was closed. He'd carved her the most beautiful set of ink pens she'd ever seen in her life, and he'd sent a year's supply of refill cartridges with them.

The more she got to know him, the more she knew she was falling in love. How could she not? If he were only half of who she believed he was, he'd still deserve to steal her heart. She hoped her heart was worthy. Even in the letter he'd given her at his home, he'd written things as deep and personal as she had written to him before she knew who he was. And she knew he truly was the man she'd thought him to be through his letters.

Lillian Petersheim walked into the office with a small stack of twenty-dollar bills in her hand and closed the door behind her.

"Hang on, Jonah." Beth held out her hand for the cash and counted it. "What do you need?"

"Ones and fives."

Beth went to the safe.

Jonah had been in the area on lumberyard business last weekend—pricing the clearing of timber from nearby land—and he and his brother had dropped by the store. Unfortunately she'd missed his visit. She and Gloria had gone into Lancaster to handle a supply-and-demand issue that needed Beth's attention firsthand.

It still struck her as odd—and heartwarming—that he didn't seem the least bit frustrated about not seeing her. Instead, he seemed to enjoy staying for dinner at Lizzy's. Her aunt sent word to Beth's parents, and they came over as well and spent the whole evening getting to know Beth's carver. Her easygoing Daed grilled Jonah and came to the conclusion he really liked him. That reassured her, but on occasion Beth still found doubt and fear lurking inside her.

She passed the bills to Lillian and picked up the receiver. "You still there?"

"Yep," Jonah replied. "In Ohio. And the question on the table is, will you join me here for Christmas?"

Silence reigned, but she was no longer surprised by his willingness to wait for her to find a voice for her thoughts. She wasn't sure she was ready to meet his family. That would shift their relationship from friendship into expectations of marriage.

If they lived in the same area, they could see each other on Christmas or any other day without anyone thinking much about it. More than likely they'd ride home together after singings; at other times he'd bring his rig to the edge of her property so she could slip off to meet him without anyone knowing. If Jonah lived close, they'd have the same friends and would have gathered for games at rotating houses, no matter what the season. That's the way courtships usually worked, allowing singles the opportunity to socialize without it meaning a declaration to marry. But when a young woman traveled four hours on Christmas Eve to see a man, it would cling to the family members like molasses—making everything it touched sticky and altering its flavor.

"Beth." Jonah's assuring voice finally broke the stillness. "If you're not at ease about this, we'll visit another time."

She'd expected him to pick up on her reluctance. He seemed to know her well, which only strengthened people's ability to hide their true self and manipulate others, didn't it? She cringed at the distrust that still crept from a hiding place and tried to rule her.

Regardless of her issues, it hurt to imagine how he must feel, knowing she wasn't returning the invitation. "I…I'm sorry, Jonah."

"Not a problem. But it's an open invitation."

"You don't mind?"

"Not if it takes a decade. Well…let's make that half a decade."

And as she said good-bye, she recognized another piece of her hesitation. She'd have to give up the business she helped build, and she didn't know if they'd ever find a solution she could live with.

Beth helped the last customer to her car, her arms full of packages. She closed the trunk and refused the tip the lady offered.

Snow swirled through the air, dulling visibility as the woman's red taillights faded into the distance. Beth couldn't remember the last time it snowed during Christmas. She buttoned her woolen coat. The glow from Lizzy's house across the street—kerosene lanterns, gas pole lamps, and the fireplace—shone clearly against the gray and white of the snowy midday.

For days her longing for Jonah had increased during every lull, and now that the store was closed for Christmas, the rest of the holiday would be one long roar of silence.

An hour ago she'd given the sales help their bonuses and sent them home. They wouldn't return until the store opened on Monday. Lizzy hadn't come in at all that day. She and Beth's Mamm were busy baking the Christmas Eve meal for most of the Hertzler clan.

As Beth stood watching Lizzy's home, she noticed Omar's carriage. His horse wasn't attached to the rig, indicating he hadn't stopped for a quick visit. Clearly he intended to spend hours at Lizzy's with Beth's family. And it dawned on her what she should have known months ago—her aunt and the bishop were more than friends.

Darkness and freezing temperatures surrounded Beth as fear of life and love tried to tighten its grip again. At thirty-eight years old her aunt had the courage to open her heart to a man who'd once been happily married, who, as bishop, bore a heavy responsibility before God, and who had a grown family and grandchildren. She guessed that he was eight years older than Lizzy. The whole situation sounded very scary to Beth.

She moved to the store's porch steps, dusted snow off, and took a seat. Why did concerns and fears constantly try to overrule her belief that love was worth it?

Thoughts and dreams and hopes swirled inside her. If she had faith instead of nagging fears, she'd find a way to get to Jonah's, even if she didn't arrive until midnight. She wouldn't worry about how much the gesture would reveal or what his family would expect from the relationship. She'd simply go and enjoy and let life be filled with unexpected moments.

"Dear God...I want what sounds so simple and feels so impossible—to trust in Jonah, in myself...in love...in You."

Several thoughts rushed through her. Pieces of Bible verses drifted first one direction and then another, like the downy flakes in front of her. Memories of the parable about the man who'd been given only one talent—one piece of money—and hid it, afraid of losing what little he'd been given, came to her. The idea of the man receiving something of value from God shook her. Was anything more important to God than love? Giving it. Accepting it. Investing it. She couldn't recall a time when He ever hinted it should be buried.

The man in the parable hid his value out of fear. *That* she understood, and once again she determined to stop. If Jonah had refused to keep moving because of his injury and pain, he'd never have carved that piece she'd discovered. He kept moving regardless of the pain, and it seemed she shouldn't keep her life on hold because rogue fears cropped up here and there.

Ready to embrace all of life, she went inside the store and called Gloria. After making plans and packing, she went to Lizzy's.

While waiting for Gloria to arrive, Beth talked with her family and exchanged gifts. Lizzy and Omar couldn't keep their eyes off each other. Lizzy caught Beth watching them and gestured toward the bedroom. Beth followed her.

Lizzy had barely passed through the doorway when she turned. "I…I wanted to tell you something. Omar asked me to marry him this afternoon."

"Hmm, he's still here, and the two of you are glowing, so I guess you said yes."

"We've been talking about it for a while, but he officially asked today. I told him you had to be the first to know. Can you believe I've finally found love?"

Tears stung Beth's eyes, and she hugged her aunt tightly. Lizzy had carried unspoken aches for years. Arm in arm they left the room.

"Ah, you told her," Omar said softly.

"Ya." Lizzy stared into his eyes. Beth headed for the living room to give them a moment of privacy. When she looked back, her aunt and the bishop stood toe-to-toe, holding hands and whispering things no one else would ever know. Omar kissed Lizzy on the cheek, and Beth wondered if they might marry before the wedding season. The rules altered for those who'd lost a spouse; they could marry whenever they wanted. Omar had been single for many years, and Beth knew he'd cherish Lizzy as the great find she was.

An hour later Beth sat in the passenger's seat of Gloria's van, waving to her family as she and Gloria pulled out of Lizzy's driveway. Snow continued to fall throughout the long, quiet drive, and Beth gazed out the window while chatting with Gloria. It felt magical to have snow on Christmas, but she wished it would stop.

The weather continued to slow their drive on Highway 22, but a little over four hours into the trip, Gloria merged into the far right lane to cross the Fort Steuben Bridge.

"I hope your surprise visit doesn't work out for you like it did for Jonah," she said.

"It won't," Beth replied. "He said the Kinsinger family spends Christmas Eve at his grandparents' place, although he goes to Pete's for a while first."

"Maybe we should stop by there on our way, just to be sure."

"Sounds like a good idea."

Brake lights shone through the white fog ahead of them, and the van fishtailed as Gloria brought it to a halt, barely missing the vehicle in front of them. Surely they could make it all the way to Jonah's. It was only fifteen, maybe twenty, more miles, but unease made Beth's skin tingle.

Beth looked behind them. Three or four cars almost locked

bumpers before regaining control. Ahead of them, traffic on the bridge was barely moving.

Gloria craned her neck, trying to see beyond the cars in front of them. "If the snow gets any thicker, we may both be staying with his grandparents tonight."

"I really don't think you should try to go back tonight. Will staying be a problem?"

"Ronnie won't be home until suppertime tomorrow. I'd like to be there in time to have a Christmas meal waiting. This is supposed to let up by morning, so we're good."

"Is it hard having a truck driver for a husband?"

Gloria wrinkled her nose. "Honey, *anything* can be hard—having a husband gone all the time, or underfoot all the time, or no husband, or…whatever. The answer is to build a life around those things. If I sat around waiting on him, I'd get unhappy. So would he. If he gets home tomorrow and I'm not there, he'll start supper, knowing I don't get mad when he's gone and he needs to return the favor. It works."

They slowly inched across the bridge and continued on Highway 22 until the Ohio River was miles behind them. Just as Beth started to relax, brake lights flashed ahead of them, and a couple of cars slid off the road. The sound of metal crunching made Beth's stomach lurch, but Gloria managed to stay on the road as she stopped the van.

"What happened?" Beth asked.

"Not sure, but it doesn't look good." Gloria turned on the radio. "Maybe there will be a report."

The minutes inched along almost as slowly as the cars crammed together on the highway. Finally a traffic report let them know a tractor-trailer had jackknifed miles ahead of them.

Even as they crept onward, Beth knew what they had to do. Once they turned off Highway 22 and began driving the back roads that lead to Tracing, the journey could be even more unpredictable.

She stared at the snow-covered roads. It seemed wrong that an object as feathery light as a snowflake could collect into something keeping her from Jonah, especially when she was this close.

"Gloria, we can't keep trying to ignore the weather. We need to find a motel."

Gloria sighed. "I think you're right. But with this weather, an empty room may not be as easy to find as it sounds."

Beth studied an information sign ahead, trying to read what hotels might be close. "It'll be easier to deal with than getting stranded in a ditch."

Nineteen

*L*ike every Christmas Eve, before going to his grandparents' house, Jonah sat across the table from Pete. But tonight Jonah stayed longer than normal, hoping to hear from Beth. He'd called her, but twice the phone was busy, and since then no one had answered. She'd be with her family by now, and he should leave. He knew that. Still…

"Care for a game of chess?" he asked.

Pete's day-old whiskers formed odd patches as he smiled. "Think you got the Christmas magic on your side this year?"

"Nope, but I'm all for giving an old man a break once in a while."

"Giving an old man…" Pete leaned across the table. "Listen here, Jonah Kinsinger, you're the Old Man."

"Then give me a break. And stop calling me Old Man in front of other people. It's caused me nothing but grief lately."

The phone rang, and Jonah almost knocked the table over jumping up to answer it.

Pete laughed. "You're right. You don't have an ounce of Christmas magic in you."

Jonah hurried into the store, glanced at the caller ID, and grabbed the phone. "Merry Christmas. I was hoping you'd call."

"Probably not hoping *I'd* call," Lizzy said.

"Well, Merry Christmas to you too, Lizzy, but I was hoping you were Beth."

"I figured that the first time we met."

Jonah chuckled. "Where is she?"

"In Ohio, stranded in a motel off Highway 22."

"She went somewhere on business on Christmas Eve? In this weather?"

"No. She went to see you."

"Me?" As the news sank in, he felt he housed the excitement of Christmas.

"The two of you need some serious help with your romantic gestures, which is why I'm intervening. I thought Pete might own a tractor or you might have some way of reaching her."

He wasn't sure he did have a way to get to her. He didn't know anyone who owned a tractor. He had a sleigh, but it needed a specific type of snow to work. "Do you know what motel she's in and where?"

While Lizzy shared the info, Jonah took notes.

"I'll give it try. Merry Christmas, Lizzy."

"Merry Christmas."

Beth looked at the small, dreary motel room. Concrete block walls, cold stale air, and the tinny sound of the cheap television Gloria was watching made the disappointment sting even more. Blasts of frigid air found their way around the door that led directly outside. She removed the pins from her prayer Kapp and bun and, unwinding her hair, sat on the edge of the bed.

Gloria held out a small bag of chips. "It's all the vending machine had left."

Beth shook her head. "They're all yours." With her coat still on, she slid between the cold sheets and pulled a blanket over her head. Gloria flipped from one news station to another.

Though she didn't feel sleepy at all, Beth closed her eyes anyway. When the sound of sleigh bells jingled over an anchorman's voice, she figured she must be sleepier than she'd thought.

The television went silent. "Did you hear that?" Gloria asked. "Santa must be coming to this old motel."

Beth sat up. "You hear sleigh bells too?"

"Sure do."

They moved to the window, but the frost kept them from seeing outside. Gloria shrugged and returned to watching television. Beth slid into her boots and added a wool scarf over her head before she opened the door. A blast of freezing air ripped through the room, stealing what little heat they had. She stepped outside and closed the door behind her.

The sound of sleigh bells rode on the night air like magic, and she looked in the direction the noise came from. She expected to see a dad in a red suit playing Santa for his stranded children on Christmas Eve, but no one came into sight.

As she listened, she realized the sound was coming from the back side of the motel.

She closed her eyes, letting the snow drift around her as she remembered so many childhood years of dreams and hopes. Memories of all the times her Daed came up with a substitute for a sleigh ride warmed her. The longer the sound went on, the lighter her heart felt. So her plan to see Jonah hadn't worked. This was a substitute year, but now that she fully trusted him and knew she loved him, they'd fulfill the real dream soon.

She opened her eyes. Through the dark night and white cloud of swirling snow, she saw a horse pulling a black sleigh with an Amish driver.

Is it possible?

Beth blinked.

Jonah.

Her heart pounded madly. Jonah pulled on the reins and slowed the horse until the sleigh came to a halt. He looked straight at her, and her mind jammed with too many thoughts to process.

His beautiful smile didn't say nearly as much as his brown eyes. "Merry Christmas."

Tears brimmed, and she couldn't find her voice.

"I knew if I kept circling the motel, you'd come outside." He held out a basket. "My mother sent dinner."

She moved closer and took the basket. The aroma of a Christmas feast filled her.

"Of course, you're welcome to come home with me." He patted the seat beside him. "Or we can stay here and eat…if I'm invited."

Stay here?

Beth shook her head. "No. I mean, yes. But…but no."

He laughed.

She drew a deep breath. "You're invited to stay, but I'd much rather you go. I…I mean…taking me with you, of course. Oh, and Gloria too."

He leaned forward. "Are you rattled, Beth Hertzler?"

She nodded, and tears warmed her cheeks. Was she dreaming? "How…"

"Lizzy called Pete. I just happened to be there…waiting and wishing you'd call."

In her mind's eye she saw children in the sleigh—just for a moment. She heard their laughter, but she couldn't tell how many of them there were. She saw a white prayer Kapp or two and a couple of black felt hats. In that moment she understood why she'd begun hearing the sleigh bells of her childhood again. For her, it was the sound of hope and love. It rang inside her as she slept, trying to remind her that love was alive and worth whatever it took to hear it when awake. But she couldn't have started hearing them again without Jonah.

An overnight bag sailed above her head, and Jonah caught it. Gloria took the basket of food from Beth. "I'll keep this. You go."

Jonah placed the bag on his far side. "You're welcome to join us," he said to Gloria.

"No thanks. I'll turn in early and hit the main roads first thing tomorrow. I have a feast to hold me over until then. I'll come back for her on Sunday." Gloria passed Beth her prayer Kapp and pins. "You enjoy your Christmas."

Beth hugged her. "I will. Thank you for this, and call Lizzy for me. I'm sure she's sitting by the phone in the office, waiting to hear what happened."

"I will."

Beth climbed into the sleigh. Jonah lifted a blanket, and she slid in beside him. The seat, as well as the blankets, was warm. She looked at Jonah for an explanation. He showed her the power source for the two electric blankets—a converted car battery.

"Pete loaned me the blankets. I had the rest." He made a clicking sound with his tongue, and the horse moved off, gaining speed.

Within minutes they were beyond all signs of town life. As they glided along the back roads, going up and down the hills that dominated the area, Jonah told her where the sleigh came from and why it was ready for use that night.

He then slowly shared his secret—the pain of resenting his siblings, Amos most of all, as Jonah suffered surgery after surgery. And the horrid, guilt-filled days when he felt like he wouldn't have saved any of them if given the same situation again.

Beth studied the man beside her, needing to hear every word he shared. "When Henry died, it was easy to forgive him. But how did you get past the pain to deal with your anger and resentment against Amos?"

"Well, time and medicine and family would have eventually helped, but during the worst of it, I caught a glimpse of how Jesus let go of His anger. Just a fraction of a second, mind you, but I saw Him on the cross, looking beyond the people who'd put Him there and to the Father He trusted. It seemed that He didn't hold the people accountable because He wasn't looking at them. When in the worst pain, He kept his focus on everything above."

His words circled inside her, and she snuggled closer. They passed through the small town where Pete's store was located and continued on toward Jonah's.

The batteries ran out of energy, and the blankets stopped giving off heat. The wind chill grew bitter. When Beth shivered, Jonah urged the horse to go faster. Soon he pulled into his driveway and headed for his home.

"You're awfully quiet, Beth. I don't think you've strung two sentences together since I arrived."

The fields were covered in snow that wouldn't melt for months yet, but the land underneath would respond to the first signs of spring, and it would become rich with nutrients as the snow slowly melted.

How could she share all that was in her mind and heart?

Jonah stopped the sleigh in front of his house. She caressed his cold cheek with the palm of her hand, wishing he could read her mind.

He studied her. "I won't forget the gift of you being here for Christmas." He moved in close, and she was sure he was going to kiss her.

"Jonah!" a man yelled.

She jolted, and Jonah smiled. "It's just my brother. When it comes to us, he has really bad timing."

"Will he always?"

"Always?" Removing the blankets, Jonah stood. "Did those words hint of a promise?"

Beth nodded.

He stepped out of the sleigh and helped her down. "Is it too soon to ask?"

She shook her head, and his smile seemed warmer than a hearth at Christmas.

Amos barreled toward them. "I'll take care of the horse. The womenfolk insisted we clear a path from your cabin to Mammi's, so you now owe us."

Beth pulled the woolen scarf tighter around her head, suddenly uncomfortable without her hair pinned up or her prayer Kapp on.

"I'll pay you guys back. Don't you worry about that." The mocking threat on Jonah's face spoke of his deep friendship with his eldest brother. "Amos, this is Beth Hertzler. I do believe she might be around quite a bit in the future if you don't scare her off."

Amos shook her hand, looking like his huge grin might soon give way to tears. Then he poked Jonah. "Me? What about you?"

"Take the horse and go." Jonah lifted her overnight bag from the sleigh. "I have something I need to ask Beth."

Amos took the reins. "I started a fire in the fireplace and in the wood stove in your bedroom more than an hour ago. Got coffee started a few minutes ago and lit a lamp in each room."

"Now that was useful. Thanks."

Jonah planted the end of his cane firmly into snow. With her overnight bag in one hand and his cane in the other, they went up the steps and into the cabin. The warmth of the room made her body ache from cold, but the place felt like a dreamland.

Jonah held her bag, looking completely at ease. "I'm not sure where you'd rather stay tonight. You're welcome to sleep here, if you won't get lonely, or at Mammi's."

"Here, if you don't mind."

"Here it is. I haven't stayed at Mammi's since I was a teen. She'll enjoy this." He carried her bag down a hallway.

Beth followed him but stopped long enough to peer into two empty rooms along the way. Neither had one stick of furniture or anything else in them, but they were bedrooms. She was sure of it. One for girls and one for boys. He'd built this house in the hope of having a family.

He stepped into a large bedroom and set her things on the bed. "The wood stove at the foot of the bed will keep it warm all night."

Looking at the exposed beams, she tugged at the oversize scarf on her head, loosening it, but keeping it on. "This is so gorgeous."

When he turned to face her, she gazed into his brown eyes, a little uncomfortable at the desire that ran between them.

His face told her he felt the same power. "I'll check on the coffee while you get settled in."

As the soft thump of his cane moved across the wooden floor and down the hallway, she longed to hear that sound every day for the rest of her life. Slowly running her hand along the rough-hewn logs of the cabin's walls, she left the bedroom and headed down the hall. "Jonah?"

He stopped at the end of the hallway.

"This whole place feels like you…I mean, like the carvings."

"Not everyone would think that's a great thing, you know," he teased.

"I'd never ask you to leave it."

"You don't have to ask. I've already decided. Home will be in Pennsylvania."

"You're part of a family-owned business."

"I've been mulling that over lately, and now I've got my eye on a cousin of mine who for years has made ends meet doing odd jobs. He's even worked at the mill when we've needed help, and I feel certain he'd jump at a chance to work at the lumbermill full-time."

"But you built this house expecting to always live here."

He moved closer, and her heart thumped like a dozen racing horses. "I can build another one, and I have no shortage of siblings willing to buy or rent it. Or, if we economize a bit, we could keep it for visits." He slowly reached for her hair, which cascaded from the loosely worn shawl that covered her head. His eyes moved over her face as he rubbed a lock between his fingers.

Suddenly aware of the quiet, empty home surrounding them, Beth eased back a step.

Jonah cleared his throat. "You should pin yourself together and join me in the living room."

Her cheeks burned, but she managed a nod. When her hair was in place and her prayer Kapp on, she walked down the hallway.

Jonah held a cup of coffee out to her. "I can't believe you're here."

"That sleigh ride…" She lifted the mug from his hand, but it was the man she drank in. "It was beyond all my best dreams."

"I was leery of driving a sleigh, but it turned out moderately worth it." He gave her a lopsided grin.

She lowered her eyes and took a sip of her drink. Did he know how much he stirred her—how he reached into the most hidden, dark parts of her soul and brought light and warmth?

He eased the mug from her hands, set it on the countertop, and stepped within an inch of her. "I love you, Beth. Everything I know about you. Everything I don't know. I love *you*." He intertwined his fingers with hers. "Will you marry me?"

Feeling a bit dizzy, she nodded. He lowered his face to hers. Within a breath of her, he paused, and then he gently pressed his lips against hers.

Her whole body trembled, and he pulled her into a hug, holding her as if she were a delicately wrapped gift. "You won't make me wait too long, will you?"

"I'd marry you today if I could."

He took a step back. "You surprise me, Beth."

"Me too."

He smiled that gentle, calm smile of his. And then he kissed her.

There was a loud knock on the door, and Amos hollered, "Coming in."

Beth's cheeks burned as she and Jonah put space between them. While Amos shut the front door, she peered up at Jonah and drew a shaky breath. "Pennsylvania, Jonah," she whispered. "Definitely, Pennsylvania is the place to live."

Jonah laughed. "That's what I said. That way your friends can break our windows instead of knocking on our door."

They laughed.

"Kumm." Jonah held out his hand. "It's time you met the rest of my family."

About the Author

CINDY WOODSMALL is a *New York Times* best-selling author. Her ability to authentically capture the heart of her characters comes from her friendships among the Old Order Amish. Cindy is the mother of three sons and two daughters-in-law, and she and her husband reside in Georgia.

Don't miss Cindy Woodsmall's
Sisters of the Quilt series

Meet Hannah Lapp, a young Amish woman whose life was transformed by a horrible tragedy, forcing her to flee the Plain life in disgrace. Wounded by her family and doubted by her fiancé, she struggles to figure out where her heart truly belongs. Be captivated by this trilogy of novels richly textured with details of Old Order Amish life and the twists and turns of authentic human relationships.

Available in bookstores and from online retailers.